# Hieroglyphics

## *And Other Stories*

## Anne Donovan

CANONGATE

First published in Great Britain in 2001 by
Canongate Books Ltd, 14 High Street,
Edinburgh EH1 1TE

1  3  5  7  9  10  8  6  4  2

These stories originally appeared in the following publications: 'Loast',
*Full Strength Angels: New Writing Scotland 14*, ASLS, 1996;
'Hieroglyphics', *Flamingo Book of New Scottish Writing*, HarperCollins,
1997; 'All That Glisters', *Scotland on Sunday*, 1997; 'Dear Santa' *Some
Sort of Embrace: New Writing Scotland 15*, ASLS, 1997; 'Wanny the
Lassies', *West Coast Magazine 28*, 1998; 'A Ringin Frost', *Chapman*, vol.
3, February 1999; 'A Chitterin Bite', *Friends and Kangaroos: New
Writing Scotland 17*, ASLS, 1999; 'A Change of Hert', *Across the Water*,
Argyll, July 2000; 'The Ice Horse', *Sunday Herald*, 2000

The author would like to thank the Scottish Arts Council for
a bursary which helped her to complete this book

The publishers gratefully acknowledge subsidy from the
Scottish Arts Council towards the publication of this volume

*British Library Cataloguing-in-Publication Data*
A catalogue record for this book is available
on request from the British Library

ISBN 1 84195 109 9

Typeset by Patty Rennie Production, Glenbervie
Printed and bound by CPD, Ebbw Vale, Wales

www.canongate.net

*For Colum, with love*

# CONTENTS

A big thank you to everyone who has given me
support and encouragement along the way

# HIEROGLYPHICS

Ah mind they were birlin and dancin roond like big black spiders. Ah couldnae keep a haunle on them fur every time ah thoat ah'd captured them, tied them thegither in some kindy order, they jist kept on escapin.

*Just learn the rules, pet. Just learn them off by heart.*

But they didnae follow oany rules that ah could make sense of. M-A-R-Y. That's ma name. Merry. But that wus spelt different fae Merry Christmas that you wrote in the cards you made oot a folded up bits a cardboard an yon glittery stuff that comes in thae wee tubes. You pit the glue on the card and shake the glitter and it's supposed tae stick in a nice wee design. It wisnae ma fault, ah didnae mean tae drap the whole load ae it on the flerr. But how come flerr wisnae spelt the same as merry and sterr wis different again and ma heid wis nippin wi coff and laff and though and bow, meanin a bit aff a tree. Ah thoat it wis Miss Mackay that wis aff her tree, right enough.

*A pride of lions*
*A gaggle of geese*
*A flock of sheep*
*A plague of locusts*

We hud tae learn aw they collective nouns aff by hert, chantin roond the class every afternoon when we came back in fae wur dinner, sittin wi oor airms foldit lookin oot the high windaes at the grey bloacks a flats and the grey streets, and sometimes the sky wisnae grey but maistly it wis. And ah could of tellt you the collective noun for every bliddy animal in the world practically, but it wis a bitty a waste when you think on it. Ah mean it would of come in handy if Drumchapel ever got overrun wi lions. You could of lookt oot the windae at some big hairy orange beast devourin yer wee sister and turn to yer mammy and say,

*Look, mammy, oor Catherine's been et by a pride of lions*

and huv the comfort a knowin ye were usin the correct terminology, but ah huv tae tell you it never happened. No even a floacky sheep ever meandered doon Kinfauns Drive of a Friday evenin (complete wi Mary and her little lamb who had mistaken their way). In fact, ah never seen any animals barrin Alsatian dugs and scabby auld cats till the trip tae the Calderpark Zoo in Primary Four.

*She lacks concentration.*
*She's lazy, ye mean.*
*No, I don't think she's lazy, there is a genuine difficulty there.*
*She's eight year auld an she canny read nor write yet.*

Ma mammy thoat ah wis daft, naw, no daft exactly, no the way wee Helen fae doon the street wis. Ah mean she didnae even go tae the same school as us an she couldnae talk right an she looked at ye funny and aw the weans tried tae avoid playin wi her in the street. Ma mammy knew ah could go the messages an dae stuff roond the hoose and talk tae folk, ah wis jist daft at school subjects, the wans that involved readin or writin oanyway. Fur a while efter she went up tae see the teacher ah got some extra lessons aff the remmy wumman but ah hated it. She wis nice tae me at furst but then when ah couldnae dae the hings she wis geein me

2

she began tae get a bit scunnered. A hink she thoat ah wis lazy, and ah could never tell them aboot the letters diddlin aboot, and oanyway, naebdy ever asked me whit it wis like. They gave me aw these tests an heard ma readin and tellt ma ma ah hud a readin age of 6.4 an a spellin age of 5.7 and Goad knows whit else, but naebdy ever asked me whit wis gaun oan in ma heid. So ah never tellt them.

And efter a while the extra lessons stoaped. They were dead nice tae me at school but. Maisty the time the teacher gied me the colourin in tae dae an when ah wis in Primary Seven ah goat tae run aw the messages an helped oot wi the wee wans. No wi their readin of course, but gettin their paints mixed an takin them tae the toilet an pittin oot the mulk fur them.

*Mary is so good with the younger children, I don't know what I'm going to do without my little assistant when she goes to the High School.*

A big rid brick buildin bloackin oot the sky. Spiky railins wi green paint peelin aff them. Hard grey tarmac space wi weans loupin aw ower the place, playin chasies in the yerd, joukin aboot roond the teachers' motors; the big yins, sophisticated, hingin aboot the corner, huvin a fly puff afore the bell goes. And us, wee furst years, aw shiny an poalished-lookin in wur new uniforms (soon tae be discardit), staunin in front ae the main door, waitin tae be tellt where we're gaun.

*Just copy the class rules off the board into your jotter.*

Anither brand new jotter. Anither set a rules tae copy. This is the last period a the day and the sixth time ah've hud tae dae it. Could they no jist huv wan lot a rules fur every class? It takes me that long tae copy the rules oot that the lesson's nearly finished and ah've missed it. The French teacher took wan look at the dug's dinner ah wis producin an tellt me no tae bother. And the Maths teacher asked me ma name an looked me up in a list.

*You're Mary Ryan, are you? Mmm.*

Must of been the remmy list. Ah'm no remmy at Maths right enough – it's jist ah cannae read the stuff. If sumbdy tells me whit tae dae ah kin usually dae it, ah jist cannae read it masel in thae wee booklets. It's funny how the numbers never seem tae birl aroond the way the letters dae; mibby it's because there urny usually as many numbers in a number as there are letters in a word, if ye know whit ah mean. Or is it because ye read them across the way and ye dae Maths doon the way? Mibby if     ah lived in wanny thae countries where they wrote doon the way ah'd be aw right. Ah mean no everybdy writes like we dae. We done a project on it in Primary Five and there's aw kinds a ways a writin in the world. Some folk read right tae left and some up and doon. And they Egyptians drew wee pictures fur aw their writin. Ah hink ah should of been an Egyptian.

*And what's this supposed to be – hieroglyphics?*

Ah hated that sarky bastard. Mr Kelly. Skelly, we cried him though he wisnae actually skelly; he used tae squint at ye through wan eye as if he wis examinin ye through a microscope an hid jist discovered some new strain a bacteria that could wipe oot the entire population a Glesga. He wis the Latin teacher but he hud hardly oany classes because naebdy done Latin noo so they'd gied him oor class fur English, and then every time a teacher wis aff sick he used tae take the class, so ah began seein a loaty him. And that wis bad news.

Ye see ah'd never felt like this afore wi oany ither teachers. Ah knew whit they were thinkin of me right enough, ah could see it in their eyes, but maisty them jist thoat ah wis a poor wee sowl that couldnae learn oanythin, so whit wis the point a them tryin ae teach me? Sometimes they even said it oot loud, like when the heidie wis daein his wee dauner roon the classes tae make sure we were aw workin hard and no writin graffiti on wer jotters. (Chance wid of been a fine thing.)

*And how are they settling in, Miss Niven?*

*Oh very well, Mr McIver, they're all working very hard on their project on the Egyptians. Amir has produced a wonderful imaginative piece on the last thoughts of Tutenkhamun and look how neatly Mary's coloured in the borders of the wall display.*

*She's a poor wee soul but she tries very hard.*

Obviously no bein able tae read makes ye deif.

But that big skelly bastard wis different. Tae start wi ah thoat he wis jist borin and boredom is sumpn that disnae bother me, ah'm used tae it, ah hink maist weans are. The furst few days he rambled on aboot grammar and wrote stuff up on the board an we didnae really huvty dae oanythin bar keep oor mooths shut. Which is easie-peesie tae me. But then he startit tae dictate notes tae us and he could time his pace jist so. If ye kin imagine the class like a field a racehorses then he wus gaun at such a pelt that only the furst two or three could keep up wi him. The rest wur scribblin furiously, their airms hingin oot thur soackets, sighin an moanin ower their jotters, and then he'd tease them wi a pause that wis jist a toty bit aff bein long enough tae let them catch up, an then, wheech, he wis aff again lik lightnin.

Me, ah wis the wan that fell at the furst fence.

Ah did try but ah goat masel intae such a complete fankle that ah hud tae stop writin, and insteid a bein like the ither teachers and jist leavin me in peace or sendin me a message or sumpn he hud tae make hissel smart by drawin attention tae me. Jist a big wean really, though it didnae feel that way at the time.

*Do you know what hieroglyphics are, Mary?*

*Aye, sur. It's Egyptian writing.*

*Yes, sir, not Aye, sir. I is the first person nominative, not that any of you will know what that means, of course, since you no longer have the good fortune to be properly educated in the classical tradition. Maybe if you would learn to speak properly you could then write properly.*

The class were aw sittin up like circus lions at this point, wonderin whit the ringmaister wis gonnae dae next. Sometimes he would launch intae a big long speech and then ye didnae huv tae dae oany work. Which wis hunky-dory as long as you wereny the wan he'd lamped oanty.

*So, Mary, if hieroglyphics means Egyptian writing, why do you think I am referring to your script using that term?*

*Because you cannae . . . can't read it, sur.*

*Precisely, Mary. And since the function of reading is to communicate, what point is there in writing something which is utterly unintelligible?*

Ah jist sat there.

*Well, Mary, I'm awaiting your answer.*

*But if you were an Egyptian you could read hieroglyphics, sur.*

*Are you trying to be funny, girl?*

*No, sur.*

*I thought not. Well, Mary, since neither you nor I nor anyone in this room appears to hail from ancient Egypt, you are going to have to learn to write in a legible hand. And since you have not managed to write down today's notes then I suggest you borrow someone else's jotter and copy them out tonight.*

Ah wis mortified, pure mortified. The lassie next tae me passed her jotter ower wioot sayin a word and ah pit it in ma bag and walked oot the room. And from that day sumpn funny startit tae happen that ah couldnae unnerstaun. The class stopped talkin tae me but it wisnae like they'd aw fell oot wi me; ah mean if ah asked tae borrow their Tipp-ex or said did ye see *Home and Away* last night, they wid answer me, but they widnae say much and they never startit a conversation wi me. And there seemed tae be an empty space aw roond me in the class, fur naebdy sat next tae me if they could help it. Ah couldnae figure it oot, fur they aw hatit auld Skelly, so how come jist because he didnae like me they didnae either. You'd hink it wid be the ither way roond.

And it wisnae jist in his class either, ah could of unnerstood that aw right fur who wants tae sit near the target practice? But it wis in every class, and the playgrund and the dinner school. And when ye move up tae the big school it's a time when friendships kindy shuffle roond like wanny they progressive barn dances, and ye make new wans an ye lose auld wans and somehow in the middly aw this process ah fund masel oot the dance wioot a partner. And it wisnae nice.

Then ah startit daein the hieroglyphics fur real. In the beginnin it wis part of oor History project on the Egyptians. We hud tae make up oor ain version, writin wee messages and stories. Miss Niven presented it tae us as if it wis some crackin new original idea, though of course we done it in Primary Four (but we didnae tell her that cos it wis better than readin aboot the preservation a mummies). And ah turnt oot tae be dead good at it. Somehow the wee pictures jist seemed tae come intae ma heid and it wis that easy compared tae writin words. If ye wanted tae say would you like a cup of tea?, ye jist drew a wee cupnsaucer an a mooth wi an arra pointin at it and a question mark. Nae worryin aboot whit kindy wood it wis or how many e's in tea.

And gradually ah progressed fae writin wee messages tae writin whole stories in pictures. Ah spent ages gettin them jist right and colourin them in wi felties and Miss Niven even gied me a special fine black pen fur daein the outlines. And the rest ae the class moved on tae the Second World War but ah stayed in ancient Egypt, stuck in a coarner a the room wi a pile a libry books roond me, drawin they wee sideyways people wi their big fish eyes. They used tae get buried wi aw the hings they thoat they'd need in their next life, they even took their food wi them, and it set me wonderin whit would ah huv took wi me intae ma next life, but then how would ye know whit it wis gonnae be like? It's a bit like gaun tae Ayr fur the day, will ye be runnin aboot on the beach in yer shorts or sittin in the café wearin five jumpers, watchin the rain pour doon? And if ye cannae prepare yersel fur a day at the seaside, how the hell ur ye gonnae dae it fur yer next life?

And the mair ah studied they libry books the mair ah could see things huvnae changed aw that much since the time a the Egyptians. They hud gods that were hauf-human an hauf-animal and as ah looked at their pictures ah saw the faces a ma teachers. So ah drew some gods ae ma ain. Miss Niven wus a wee tweetery wumman, aye dartin roond the classroom so ah gied her the body ae a wumman and the heid ae a wee speug, coacked tae wan side. Then there wis Mr Alexander, hauf-man, hauf-fish cos he wis aye losin the place. Auld Kelly hud grey crinkly herr lik a judge's wig and a big baw face so he hud tae be a ram wi huge curly hoarns, jist like the Egyptian god ae the underworld. Very appropriate, that. And ah wis jist tryin tae work oot whether the heidie wis mair lik the Sun god or a sphinx, when he swept intae the room.

*Miss Niven, the Quality Assurance Unit will be visiting the school next Tuesday, nothing to worry about, just an informal visit to pick out good practice.*

*Will they want to see my planning sheets?*

*Yes, but I'm sure all your paperwork is up to date, and there is evidently splendid work going on in the room. But what is this child doing drawing pictures of Egyptians? Should she not be on to the 'Victory for Democracy' unit by now?*

So the next day ma felties an cardboard were pit away and ah hud tae dae a worksheet on the Russian front. She let me keep the wee fine black pen though. She's dead nice, Miss Niven.

But Skelly Kelly wis still a bastard and ah got him every day a the week. And his teachin wisnae even as modern as the ancient Egyptians, oot the ark, mair like; aw ye did wis write, write, write till yer airm felt

like a big balloon or ye hud tae dae grammar exercises and interpreta-
tions, and he never read us stories like the ither English teachers. And
because ah couldnae dae aw the writin in time, ah ended up takin piles a
stuff hame tae copy up every night, then he took the jotters in wanst a
week and mines came back covered in red marks. Ma writin looked a bit
like wee scarab beetles scurryin aboot the page and when he corrected it,
it wis as if the wee beetles hud aw startit bleedin.

*Once again, Mary Ryan, I can barely read a word of your writing.*

Ah couldnae unnerstaun a word of whit he wrote on ma jotter either
but ah couldnae very well say that, could ah?

And then wan day ah couldnae take it oany longer.

*Today you will be doing a timed composition. This is to give you
practice for your examinations. The question is on the board. You have
precisely fifty minutes. Begin.*

Imagine you are going on a journey. Describe where you are going and
what things you would take with you.

So ah startit tae write aboot ma journey tae the next world and the hings
ah wid take wi me, aw in wee pictures. Ah drew me and ma mammy (ma
da might as well be in the next world fur aw ah see of him) and ma
sisters, Catherine an Elizabeth, in a wee boat fur ah hud some idea that
ah wanted ma journey tae be ower the watter. And we took nice stuff tae
eat, big plates a mince an tatties (ah know ye couldnae really keep them
hot but it kinda makes sense the way the Egyptians dae it) and ice cream
fae the café an bottles a ginger and sweeties and that.

Ah spent a long time thinkin oot whit else ah wanted tae take, fur a
loaty the hings we huv in this world might no be oany use tae us in the
next. After aw, whit use are CDs if there's nae electricity? So ah decided
tae gie each ae us three hings tae take in the boat fur ye widnae want that

much stuff that the boat wid sink, an oanyway three is wanny they numbers that's gey important in stories. Who ever heardy emdy gettin five wishes aff their fairy godmother or the two blind mice or seventeen wee pigs?

Elizabeth's three hings were easy fur she's only four an she aye cairries a bitty auld blanket roond wi her, and she'll no go oanywhere wioot her teddy or her Sindy doll. Catherine's eight but she would need tae take her teddy too and her new blue jumper wi a picture of a wee lamb on it an her deelie-boablers; ye know they hings ye pit roond yer heid like an Alice band but they've got wee antennas stickin oot fae them an they make ye look lik sumpn fae ooter space. Ah know these kindy hings go in and ooty fashion and two weeks fae noo she'll feel like a real chookie when she minds she wanted tae go tae mass in them, but at the moment she'd want tae take them. And ah'd take some paper and the black pen fur daein ma hieroglyphics, and ma picture ae a wee spaniel pup that ah cut oot of a magazine and keep on the wall by ma bed, fur we couldnae huv a real dug doon ma bit.

But whit would ma mammy take wi her? Aw ae a sudden it came tae me that ah didnae know whit ma mammy wid take on her journey tae the next world, it wid need tae be sumpn private and jist fur her, and mammys don't tell ye these things fur they're too busy workin and bringin ye up tae huv a loaty time fur theirsels. And then auld Kelly told us tae finish off, it wis time, so ah hud tae leave her wi naethin. But mibby no, fur ah hink if ah'd asked her, ma mammy wid say we are her three best hings; Catherine and Elizabeth and me.

*Mary Ryan will collect in the compositions.*

Ah walked roond the class, gaitherin in the bits a paper, lookin at each wan as ah picked it up. Aw they different kinds a haunwritin; squinty, straight, big or wee, different sizes and shapes on the page. Then ah picked up ma ain story wi its neat wee black drawins and noticed ah hudny pit ma name on it. So ah drew a wee picture of masel wi a cheery face on it, pit ma story right on tap ae the pile and planted the whole lot doon in the centre of his desk.

# ALL THAT GLISTERS

Thon wee wifie brung them in, the wan that took us for two days when
Mrs McDonald wis aff. She got us tae make Christmas cards wi
coloured cardboard and felties, which is a bit much when we're in
second year, but naebdy wis gonnae say anythin cos it's better than
daein real work. Anyway ah like daein things like that and made a right
neat wee card for ma daddy wi a Christmas tree and a robin and a bit a
holly on it.

*That's lovely, dear. What's your name?*

*Clare.*

*Would you like to use the glitter pens?*

And she pulled oot the pack fae her bag.

Ah'd never seen them afore. When ah wis in Primary Four the
teacher gied us tubes of glitter but it wis quite messy. Hauf the stuff
ended up on the flair and it wis hard tae make sure you got the glue in
the right places. But these pens were different cos the glue wis mixed in
wi the glitter so you could jist draw with them. It wis pure brilliant, so it
wis. There wis four colours, rid, green, gold and silver, and it took a wee
while tae get the hang of it. You had tae be careful when you squeezed
the tube so's you didnae get a big blob appearin at wanst, but efter a few
goes ah wis up an runnin.

And when ah'd finished somethin amazin hud happened. Ah cannae
explain whit it wis but the glitter jist brought everythin tae life, gleamin

and glisterin agin the flat cardboard. It wis like the difference between a Christmas tree skinklin wi fairy lights an wan lyin deid an daurk in a corner.

Ma daddy wis dead chuffed. He pit the card on the bedside table and smiled.

*Fair brightens up this room, hen.*

It's good tae find sumpn that cheers him up even a wee bit because ma daddy's really sick. He's had a cough fur as long as ah can remember, and he husny worked fur years, but these past three month he cannae even get oot his bed. Ah hear him coughin in the night sometimes and it's different fae the way he used tae cough, comes fae deeper inside him somehow, seems tae rack his hale body fae inside oot. When ah come in fae school ah go and sit wi him and tell him aboot whit's happened that day, but hauf the time he looks away fae me and stares at a patch on the downie cover where there's a coffee stain that ma ma cannae wash oot. He used tae work strippin oot buildins and he wis breathin in stour aw day, sometimes it wis that bad he'd come hame wi his hair and his claes clartit wi it. He used tae kid on he wis a ghost and walk in the hoose wi his airms stretched oot afore him and ah'd rin and hide unner the stair, watchin him walk by wi the faint powdery whiteness floatin roon his heid.

He never knew there wis asbestos in the dust, never knew a thing aboot it then, nane of them did. Noo he's an expert on it, read up aw these books tae try and unnerstaun it fur the compensation case. Before he got really sick he used tae talk aboot it sometimes.

*You see, hen, the word asbestos comes fae a Greek word that means indestructible. That's how they use it fur fireproofin – the fire cannae destroy it.*

*You mean if you wore an asbestos suit you could walk through fire and it widnae hurt you?*

*Aye. In the aulden days they used tae bury the royals in it. They cried it the funeral dress of kings.*

The next day the wee wumman let me use the pens again. Sometimes when you think somethin's brilliant it disnae last, you get fed up wi it dead quick an don't know why you wanted it in the first place. But the pens werenae like that, it wis even better than the first time cos ah knew whit tae dae wi them. Yesterday ah'd put the glitter on quite thick in a solid block a colour, but today ah found a different way a daein it almost by accident. Ah'd drawn a leaf shape and coloured it green but a bit squirted oot intae a big blob, so ah blotted it and when ah took the paper away the shape that wis left wis nicer than the wan ah'd made deliberately. The outline wis blurred and the glitter wis finer and lighter, the colour of the card showin through so it looked as if sumbdy'd sprinkled it, steidy ladelin it on; it looked crackin. The teacher thought so too.

*It's lovely, Clare. It's more . . . subtle.*

Subtle, ah liked that word.

Ah tellt ma daddy aboot it that night efter school, sittin on the chair beside his bed. He seemed a bit better than usual, mair alert, listenin tae whit ah hud tae say, but his skin wis a terrible colour and his cheeks were hollow.

*Whit did she mean, subtle, hen? How wis it subtle?*

Ah tried tae think of the words tae explain it, but ah couldnae. Ah looked at ma fingers which were covered in glitter glue and then at ma daddy's haun lyin on the bedcover, bones stickn oot and veins showin through. Ah took his haun in mines and turnt it roon so his palm faced upwards.

*Look, daddy.*

Ah showed him the middle finger of ma right haun, which wis thick wi solid gold, then pressed doon on his palm. The imprint of ma finger left sparkly wee trails a light.

He smiled, a wavery wee smile.

*Aye, hen. Subtle.*

That night ah lay awake fur a while imaginin aw the things ah could dae wi the glitter pens. Ah really wanted tae make sumpn fur ma daddy's Christmas wi them. The tips of ma fingers were still covered in glitter, and they sparkled in the daurk. Ah pressed ma fingers aw ower the bedclothes so they gleamed in the light fae the streetlamps ootside, then ah fell intae a deep glistery sleep.


£3.49 for a pack of four. And ah hud wan ninety-three in ma purse.

Ah lifted the pack and walked to the check-oot.

*Much are they?*

*Three forty-nine.*

*Aye, but much are they each?*

The wumman at the till hud dyed jet-black hair and nae eyebrows.

*We don't sell them individually.*

She spat oot the word *individually* as if it wis sumpn disgusting.

*Aye, but you'll get mair fur them. Look, you can have wan ninety-three fur two.*

*Ah've already tellt you that we don't sell them individually, ah cannae split the pack.*

Ah could see there wis nae point in arguin wi her so ah turnt roon and walked towards the shelf tae pit them back. If Donna'd been wi me, she'd just have knocked them. She's aye takin sweeties an rubbers an wee things like that. She's that casual aboot it, she can jist walk past a shelf and wheech sumpn intae her pocket afore anybdy notices, never gets caught. And she's that innocent-lookin, wi her blonde frizzy curls an her neat school uniform naebdy wid guess tae look at her she wis a tea-leaf.

She's aye on tae me tae dae it, but ah cannae. Ah suppose it's cos of ma ma and da, they're dead agin thievin. Donna widnae rob hooses or steal sumpn oot yer purse but she disnae think stealin oot a shop is stealin. A lot of folk think like that. Donna's big brother Jimmy wanst tried tae explain tae me that it wis OK tae steal ooty shops cos they made such big profits that they were really stealin affy us (the workin classes he cries us though he husny worked a day in his life) and they're aw insured anyway so it disnae matter. Even though ah can see the sense in whit Jimmy's sayin, well, ma daddy says stealin is stealin, and ah cannae go against his word.

In the end ah sellt ma dinner tickets tae big Maggie Hughes and all week ah wis starvin for ah only hud an apple or a biscuit ma ma gied me fur a playpiece. But on Friday it wis worth it when ah went doon the shops at lunchtime tae buy the pens. It wis a different wumman that served me and she smiled as she pit them in a wee plastic poke.

*Are you gonnae make Christmas decorations, hen?*

*Ah'm no sure.*

*Ah got some fur ma wee boy an he loved them.*

*Aye, they're dead good. Thanks.*

Ah couldnae wait tae show them tae ma da, but as soon as ah opened the door of the hoose ah knew there wis sumpn wrang. It wis that quiet, nae telly, nae radio on in the kitchen. Ma mammy wis sittin on the settee in the livin room. Her face wis white and there were big black lines under her eyes.

*Mammy, whit's . . .*

*C'mere, hen, sit doon beside me.*

She held her weddin ring between the thumb and first finger of her right haun, twistin it roon as she spoke and ah saw how loose it wis on her finger. No long ago it wis that tight she couldnae get it aff.

*Clare, yer daddy had a bad turn jist this afternoon and we had tae go tae the hospital wi him. Ah'm awful sorry, hen, ah don't know how tae tell you, but yer daddy's died.*

Ah knew it wis comin, ah think ah'd known since ah walked intae the hoose, but when she said the words the coldness shot through me till ah felt ma bones shiverin and ah heard a voice, far away in anither room, shoutin but the shouts were muffled as if in a fog, and the voice wis shoutin *naw, naw, naw!*

And ah knew it wis ma voice.

We sat there, ma mammy and me, her airms roon me, till ah felt the warmth of her body gradually dissolve the ice of mine. Then she spoke, quiet and soft.

*Now, hen, you know that this is fur the best, no fur us but fur yer daddy.*

Blue veins criss-crossed the back of her haun. Why were veins blue when blood wis red?

*You know yer daddy'd no been well fur a long time. He wis in a lot of pain, and he wisnae gonnae get better. At least this way he didnae suffer as much. He's at peace noo.*

We sat for a long time, no speakin, just haudin hauns.

The funeral wis on the Wednesday and the days in between were a blur of folk comin an goin, of makin sandwiches an drinkin mugs of stewed tea, sayin rosaries an pourin oot glasses of whisky for men in overcoats. His body came hame tae the hoose and wis pit in their bedroom. Ma mammy slept in the bed settee in the livin room wi ma Auntie Pauline.

*Are you sure that you want tae see him?*

Ah wis sure. Ah couldnae bear the fact we'd never said goodbye and kept goin ower and ower in ma mind whit ah'd have said tae him if ah'd known he wis gonnae die so soon. Ah wis feart as well, right enough.

Ah'd never seen a deid body afore, and ah didnae know whit tae expect, but he looked as if he wis asleep, better in fact than he'd looked when he wis alive, his face had mair colour, wis less yella lookin an lined. Ah sat wi him fur a while in the room, no sayin anythin, no even thinkin really, jist sittin. Ah felt that his goin wis incomplete and ah wanted tae dae sumpn fur him, but that's daft, whit can you dae when sumbdy's deid? Ah wondered if ah should ask ma mammy but she wis that withdrawn intae hersel, so busy wi the arrangements that ah didnae like tae. She still smiled at me but it wis a watery far-away smile and when she kissed me goodnight ah felt she wis haudin me away fae her.

On the Wednesday mornin ah got up early, got dressed and went through tae the kitchen. Ma Auntie Pauline wis sittin at the table havin a cuppa tea and a fag and when she looked up her face froze over .

*Whit the hell dae you think you're daein? Go and get changed this minute.*

*But these are ma best claes.*

*You cannae wear red tae a funeral. You have tae show respect fur the deid.*

*But these were ma daddy's favourites. He said ah looked brilliant in this.*

Ah mind his face when ah came intae the room a couple of month ago, after ma mammy'd bought me this outfit fur ma birthday; a red skirt and a zip-up jaicket wi red tights tae match.

*You're a sight fur sore eyes, hen.*

*That sounds horrible, daddy.*

He smiled at me.

*It disnae mean that, hen, it means you look that nice that you would make sore eyes feel better. Gie's a twirl, princess.*

And ah birled roon on wan leg, laughin.

\*

19

*They claes are no suitable for a funeral.*

*Ah'm gonnae ask ma mammy.*

Ah turned to go oot the room.

*Don't you dare disturb your mother on a day like this tae ask her aboot claes. Have you no sense? Clare, you're no a baby, it's time you grew up and showed some consideration for other folk. Get back in that room and put on your school skirt and sweatshirt and your navy-blue coat. And ah don't want to hear another word aboot this.*

In the bedroom ah threw masel intae a corner and howled ma heid aff. The tears kept comin and comin till ah felt ah wis squeezed dry and would never be able tae shed anither tear. Ah took aff the red claes and changed intae ma grey school skirt and sweatshirt and pit ma navy-blue coat ower it. Ah looked at masel in the full-length mirror in the middle of the wardrobe and saw this dull drab figure, skin aw peely-wally. Ma daddy would have hated tae see me like this but ah didnae dare go against ma auntie's word.

The only bit of me that had any life aboot it wis ma eyes fur the tears had washed them clean and clear. A sunbeam came through the windae and ah watched the dustspecks dancin in its light. There was a hair on the collar of ma coat and it lit up intae a rainbow of colours. As ah picked it up and held it in ma fingers, an idea came tae me. Ah went tae ma schoolbag which had been left lyin in the corner of the room since Friday, took oot ma pack of glitter pens and unwrapped them. Ah took the gold wan, squeezin the glitter on ma fingers then rubbin it intae ma hair, then added silver and red and green. The strands of hair stood oot roon ma heid like a halo, glisterin and dancin in the light. Ah covered the dull cloth so it wis bleezin wi light, patterns scattered across it, even pit some on ma tights and ma shoes. Then ah pressed ma glittery fingers on ma face, feelin ma cheekbones and eyebrows and the soft flesh of ma mouth and the delicate skin of ma eyelids. And ah felt sad for a moment as ah thought of the deid flesh of ma daddy, lyin alone in the cold church. Then ah stood and looked in the mirror at the glowin figure afore me and ah smiled.

Subtle, daddy?

Aye, hen, subtle.

# THE ICE HORSE

Even through the blanket and layers of warm clothing, Anna felt the cold penetrate her skin. Stretching across the horse's back, she reached her arms along its neck, gouging into the ice with a metal scraper. Her arms ached. A chunk of ice snapped off, revealing the misted glass body of the horse. After only a few seconds, the coating renewed itself, a frosting of icing sugar this time which wiped off as easily as dust but kept forming and re-forming. Tired of her work, she slid off the horse's back, and stood at its head. She started to polish its face, rubbing her cloth into the furrows of its curly mane and the carved detail of flared nostrils. Tentatively she touched its left eye and the film peeled off like a cataract.

Immediately the crystals of ice re-formed and the eye dimmed, though tiny sparks of light shot from the white mask. Anna knew it was pointless to continue, since it was so cold that it would keep icing over, yet she could not stop. She wanted to see the horse in his true magnificence, to rock back and forth on his broad back. Most of all, she longed to look into his eyes and hold their gaze.

The door of the shed creaked open and her mother entered. A blue mohair scarf was wound tightly round her neck, almost covering her face, and she pulled it away to speak.

'Are you still trying to clean up that old thing?'

'It's no use. It's too cold in here. Can we not bring him into the house?'

'No.'

'But he's so beautiful. He would work properly if he didn't have to stay in this freezing old shed.'

'I've told you. He has to stay here.'

She touched Anna's shoulder, her hands cocooned in quilted gloves, clumsy as oven mitts.

'Come into the house. It's tea-time.'

Anna followed her across the yard. The light had faded but snow cast a reflected brightness and the path glittered. Pausing at the doorway, Anna turned to look back across the yard to the shed.

In the kitchen, heat blasted them from the open fire. Grandfather's house was old-fashioned, very different from the one where she lived with her mother. When they came to visit, their lives were different too, following his ways.

'He's an old man,' her mother would say. 'It costs you nothing to please him.'

Grandfather was already in his place and Anna slid into the chair next to his. Her mother lifted the big pot from the stove and placed it on a metal trivet in the centre of the table. She filled bowls with soup while Anna passed round a basket of bread. When everyone was served, they began to eat.

'What have you been up to this afternoon, Anna?'

'She's been out in the shed playing with that old rocking-horse.'

'I'm not playing with him. I'm trying to clear the ice from him, but it keeps coming back.'

'You'll need to wait till this big freeze comes to an end,' said Grandfather.

'They said on the radio it won't get warmer till next week.'

Her grandfather smiled. 'And you can't wait till then?'

Anna dipped her spoon into the bowl and took a mouthful of soup. It was too hot and she could feel the roof of her mouth burning as she tried to hold the liquid there to cool before she swallowed. She knew that later the skin would come off and leave a ragged feeling in her mouth.

In her dream the horse was silver, his ice-coat shot through with a million stars. Anna swept a cloth across his side and the shell melted in an instant. She climbed on his back and lay there, felt the surface beneath start to prick like pins and needles in the rising warmth. His carved mane was transformed into soft strands, which she gripped as the horse began to move. He picked up speed and they galloped across a huge expanse of sand, ghost-white under a clouded moon. Anna clung to his back. She could hear his harsh breath, see steam issue from his nostrils. Suddenly he stopped dead and she shot over his neck, the mane wrenched from her fingers, damp sand burning her limbs as she slid along the beach; then she woke, sitting up in bed, soaked with sweat.

For a moment she could not move because of the pain, a sharpness stabbing her chest, then it grew less intense, shifting to lower down, in her belly. The edges blurred till it was an ache, dull and heavy, leaving a sick aftertaste. She pulled her pale blue dressing gown from the edge of the bed, hugging herself with it. The roof of the shed was visible through the window, patched with snow. She crept downstairs, holding her breath as she passed her mother's room, pulled on her coat and shoes, then lifted the heavy latch which secured the door. Cold air chafed her skin as she stepped outside, hurried the few steps to the shed, and opened the door.

The horse faced away from her and she waited apprehensively, expecting him to move, to speak even. But he radiated stillness, like an actor who knows that he will move, not now, but when his part requires. Anna stepped closer to look at his face, but his eyes were veiled by blinkers of ice. She put her arm round his neck, touching the side of his cheek and her fingertips stuck to its surface. She tried to pull them away but the ice clutched her tightly, then she blew hard till reluctantly it released its grip. Anna spread her hands out, examining them. Each person's fingerprints were unique. Could ice burn them off?

'Anna, what on earth? Anna . . .' Her mother's arms were round her, holding her tightly, almost dragging her up the path to the house. She pushed her down on the rug in front of the fireplace, rattling the poker in the embers, trying to raise them to life.

'You'll catch pneumonia. What on earth were you doing?'

She held Anna's hands in hers, rubbing them hard.

'I don't know, I had to see him.'

'Why, what's so important about this horse?'

'You tell me. Why can't he come in the house?'

Her mother stopped, released Anna's hands.

'What are you talking about? The horse is just a toy, a dirty old toy.'


In the morning Anna's mother drew her aside.

'I don't want you to play with the horse today.'

'But I'm not playing, I . . .'

'Whatever. I want you to spend some time with your grandfather. He likes you to help him around the place and you've hardly spoken to him the past few days. Will you do that?'

Anna looked at the ground.

'Will you?'

'Yes,' she said, without looking up.

'That's my good girl.'

Grandfather was preparing the doors in the hall for repainting; burning off old gloss paint, sanding the wood with fine paper, and putting on undercoat. Anna's mother had told him there was no need, as modern paints were designed to go on over the old stuff, but he maintained that his way gave a better finish.

'Anyway,' he smiled, 'too late to teach an old dog new tricks. Keeps me out of mischief. And you.' He turned to Anna, ruffling her hair with his hand. Anna squirmed.

Her job was to sand down the wood prepared by her grandfather. She sat on the floor working her way slowly along the bottom edge. The sandpaper rasped against the door, forming a fine coating of dust on her fingers.

Her mother came into the hall. 'I'm just going into town for some shopping. See you later.'

'Bye,' said Anna, without looking up.

'Don't forget the chocolate biscuits. I think we may be running low on supplies,' said Grandfather.

'I wonder why?' replied her mother.

Grandfather put down his scraper and stretched, linking his fingers above his head.

'I think it's time for a break, Anna. Let's put the kettle on.'

In the kitchen he made tea for himself and hot chocolate for Anna while she laid biscuits on a plate. Grandfather sat back in his chair in front of the fire and she leaned forward on a low stool at the other side of the hearth.

'D'you think we can start painting this afternoon?'

He poured his tea into a saucer, blew on it, then sipped. Anna's mother hated when he did that.

'Maybe. If we get the sanding done in time. But we have to do it properly. The preparation is the important part, Anna. If you do the preparation, the rest will follow, but if you skimp it, the job'll never be done properly, no matter how long you spend on it.'

Anna stared into the fire. Grandfather, worn out, began to doze in the heat, his head to one side, mouth slightly open. When she was sure he was asleep, Anna placed her mug on the stone hearth, crept into the hall where he had left his blowtorch, then out to the shed.

Cold air entered freely through the broken window, draughts blasted from the roof and filled gaps between the walls and stone floor. In the clear daylight the horse looked dingy and sad, ice forming a protective husk round his body. Anna crouched in front of him, holding the blowtorch in her hand. The metal felt cold even through thick gloves. She placed one finger on the rocker of the horse and it started to tap rhythmically on the floor. The rockers were made of wood, their dark varnish scuffed and scraped. Anna pressed the starter button and the flame hissed out and licked the edge of the rocker. She let it play, teasing the wood, staining it with faint scorch marks. Then she held the torch against the centre of the rocker, pressed her fingers firmly on the control till the fire took hold, flickering blue at first, then flaring orange and red. Methodically, she set fire to each end of the rocker, then repeated the process on the other side. Anna lifted a scraper and stabbed it into the horse's back, smashing the ice in a crazy-paving pattern. She tore off the pieces with her fingers, as the heat below started to make her eyes water and cheeks tingle; then she stood back, watching the lines of fire slither along the rockers, growing stronger, feeding from each other where they touched. For a moment she feared that the water dripping from the horse would put the fire out, but it slid clean onto the floor, for the most part missing the flames. Anna stretched her hand over the fire and gave the horse a push. He began to move, surging back and forward in a sea of flames, trails of vapour escaping his nostrils and rising from his mane and tail, his damp back. As the last of the ice escaped, trickling down the sides of his face, his beautiful clear eyes looked straight into Anna's.

# VIRTUAL PALS

e-mail
Date: 18.1.2001    10.25.34
From: sio2c@allan.gla.sch.uk
To: 2c@allan.jupiter.net.sch.uk

Hi,

My name is Siobhan and I am in 2C at Allan High School, Glasgow. Our English teacher is getting us to do e-mails to your school in Shetland and we have to tell you about our lifes but because everybody has to get to go on the computer we have to keep it short she says to just put in the most important stuff.

Well I am 12 coming up 13 on march 5th and I live with my mum but I stay with my dad on the weekends he stays just round the corner. I have a wee brother James aged 10 he is in p6. My pet is a cross labrador called Lucky.

Please reply soon as I want to find out all about your life.

Siobhan

e-mail

Date: 19.1.2001    03.91.24.87

From: iri2c@allan.jupiter.net

To: sio2c@allan.gla.sch.uk

Dear Siobhan,

It was somewhat surprising to receive your electronic mail since in our science lessons we have learned that the area of your planet known as Scot-land is devoid of intelligent life, due to adverse climatic conditions.

At first I was under the apprehension that I had become the victim of a practical jape and was about to report the misdemeanour to the Committee for Ethical Standards of the Jupiter Communication Information Superhighway Board. However, on further reflection, I felt I ought to reply since, if you really are a citizen of Planet Earth, this would be a wonderful discovery for my area board and a great honour for my family.

I should tell you some information about myself and my family. I, too, am 12 years old and will be 13 soon. Overpopulation on Jupiter, however, has meant that parents are only permitted one child so I do not have the good fortune of a brother. My mother is an ecologistics professor and my father is a biostratospheric technician. The language transference tool on my computer which translated your message did not recognise the word 'pet'. Perhaps in your reply you could enlighten me as to the meaning of this word.

I look forward to your reply.

Irina

e-mail
Date: 20.1.2001   10.25.34
From: sio2c@allan.gla.sch.uk
To: iri2c@allan.jupiter.net

Dear Irina,

It's pure brilliant to get your e-mail. Your letter was the best reply in the class. Everybody else is jealous they didn't get a penpal from Jupiter and Janine even said she'd gie us a signed Steps tee shirt if I'd swop with her but I'm not gonnae.

Anyway, you were asking about what a pet is. Well Lucky is a dog. A cross labrador is no a purebred labrador but has a bit of labrador in it. But a pet doesn't have to be a dog it can be a cat or a budgie or that. My granny has a budgie but that's no much of a pet it's dead boring. A dog is a good pet because you can take it out for walks and it'll protect you as well if anybody tries to give you a doin.

There was some bits in your letter that I didn't understand too. Like what your ma and da do for their jobs – I don't think we have them here. My ma works part time in the Co-op and my da is a plumber. I think you're dead lucky no having a brother, mine's is a wee pest. He wrote all over the posters in my room and my ma never even gave him into trouble because she said it was an accident she's always doing that sticking up for him just cos he's the baby.

Anyway I'll tell you some of my favourite things. My favourite food is Chinese especially pancake rolls and fried rice. My favourite band is Steps and my favourite colour is purple. What's your favourites?

31

I'm really looking forward to hearing from you.

Your pal

Siobhan

PS Miss Macintosh thought that bit about Scotland being devoid of intelligent life was dead funny. She said to tell you it's just 2C that's devoid of intelligent life, but she was joking. She thinks you're no really fae Jupiter, just a pupil at that other school kidding on. I'm no gonnae tell her.


e-mail
Date: 21.1.2001    08.57.88.93
From: iri2c@allan.jupiter.net
To: sio2c@allan.gla.sch.uk

Dear Siobhan,

I am delighted to receive your communication. It seems that you are truly a citizen of Earth. However, after consulting my parents and considering the issue carefully, I feel we should continue our correspondence for a while longer before I report the matter. If I do so now, we may not be permitted to continue, since the investigation will be transferred to a higher authority and, while I am aware that perhaps this is a slightly selfish point of view, I should like to have the opportunity to develop a greater intimacy with you. I hope that you feel the same way.

To return to the substance of your communication, I am surprised that you do not consider your brother to be a blessing; we have been taught that to have a sibling is a priceless privilege. Our mythology has many legends illustrating the joyous camaraderie of brothers and sisters and of the sacrifices they make willingly for each other. Even our constitution declares the intention that when it becomes possible, either by technological advance or some other means, Jupiterian families will be able to have more than one child.

You asked about the occupations of my mother and father. This is a complex matter which deserves a reply at greater length, so I will return to the subject in another communication.

Thank you very much for your explanation of the word 'pet'. I am still not entirely clear about your relationship with it but our encyclopaediae do contain archive pictures of dogs. However, I am baffled by the word 'favourite'. My transference tools keep bringing up the message 'no such concept', so perhaps again you would be good enough to try to explain. I feel that this correspondence is extremely educational for me.

I will use your Earth phrase to sign off.

Your pal

Irina

e-mail
Date: 24.1.2001   2.43.34
From: sio2c@allan.gla.sch.uk
To: iri2c@allan.jupiter.net


Dear Irina,


Your e-mails are just pure brilliant. I don't know how you manage to write all they big words. I have to look up a dictionary to find the meanings of half of them. Miss Macintosh is dead chuffed cos she says it's gonnae improve my English. She really liked that bit about favourites.

Favourite just means the thing you like best, like your best TV programme or colour, you know, the one you'd pick if somebody gied you a choice. Maybe now you can tell me some of yours.

You know, Irina, I'm beginning to feel that you and me are real pals and that I can trust you. I do have pals here on earth but actually there's some things I can't talk to them about because they might laugh at me or they might tell somebody else. So I'm gonnae tell you because there's something about you that makes me feel you won't laugh at me, you take everything that serious, don't you? And anyway who could you tell? If you tellt your pals on Jupiter, well then it wouldn't matter if they laughed because they don't know me.

And now's a good time for me to explain it to you cos Miss Macintosh is off sick this week and the supply teacher that's takin us is no lookin at wer e-mails, he just tellt us to get on with our work and no disturb him. I think he's reading the paper actually but he's got it hidden inside a red folder.

So I'll tell you my secret. And just in case you don't know what a secret is, it's something that if you tell someone they've no to tell anyone else, it's something just between the two of them because they're pals, special pals.

And my secret is that I really fancy Paul Wilson and sometimes I think he fancies me back too though I'm no sure, it's that hard tae tell with boys they just don't say anything. And I cannae tell Angie or Kate because Paul isnae the sort of boy that you're supposed to fancy. He's not that good-looking for a start but I think he's got gorgeous eyes. But he wears glasses and you're no supposed tae fancy boys that wear glasses either. And he's dead quiet. He's clever too.

Anyway the thing is Sharon McGhee is having a party on Saturday and she's invited everybody in our reggy class so Paul will be going and I'm so desperate to get off with him but I don't know what to do. Every time I think about it my stomach just starts churning round as if I'm going to be sick. And when I'm lying in my bed at night I sometimes imagine him coming up to me at the party and asking me to dance and slow dancing with him then he walks me home and kisses me goodnight and that's it, everything is perfect. But then I get these other pictures running through my head and there's me at the party and the next thing Paul walks through the door with this gorgeous girl who's his girlfriend and I just want to die.

So please Irina can you give me any advise about what to do?

Your pal

Siobhan

PS For your sake I hope they technological advances that will let youse have brothers don't happen too soon. Believe me, those myths are fairy tales.

e-mail
Date: 25.1.2001    07.25.34.65
From: iri2c@allan.jupiter.net
To: sio2c@allan.gla.sch.uk

Dear Siobhan,

I am delighted that you have trusted me with your confidences though I am somewhat concerned about their substance. From what you tell me about your feelings for this Paul Wilson, it appears that they are very unhealthy. In last session's Applied Psychology module we dealt with the adolescent awakening of the sexual impulse. Believe me, it is not unusual for people of our age to project their emerging energies on to another being and to imagine all sorts of qualities which they do not in fact possess. Fantasising about this boy is a waste of time. This is one of the reasons why in times past the female of the species tended to achieve less than the male, as she was programmed biologically and sociologically to a more introspective and less active resolution of her sexuality. For many centuries we on Jupiter have undergone training programmes for both genders, designed to counteract these tendencies and promote greater equality.

You ask what you should do about this boy. I would suggest that you approach him directly and, if he is willing, participate in sexual congress with him. This will put your relationship on a footing of equality and reality. Naturally you will need to protect yourself from pregnancy and disease but I understand this is quite straightforward in your culture. Should he be reluctant to participate, then simply forget him. Wishful thinking has been one of the greatest barriers to progress in every race, but particularly the human race, and I understand from my research that the human female is particularly prone to it.

You refer to matters of greater importance in your communication. I am surprised that your teacher thinks that you can learn from my English. Surely the register, vocabulary and syntax of your language is culturally and socially appropriate to your environment and the only reason for using other forms of language is that they are more fitting in a given situation? I appreciate that there are different norms within complex social groupings. (On our planet we do have differences in vocabulary between areas, for example, and some differences between generations too.) However the idea that one form of language is better than the other is foreign to our culture.

It is interesting that you introduced this idea, however, because I had intended to experiment a little with your vocabulary and syntax. At present I use a language-transference tool which has been constructed largely from the written word and from literary texts, some of which date from centuries prior to your own. (I believe this may account for a somewhat formality of tone.) Perhaps if I do so, you would tell me if I am using the correct phrases? I would be interested in compiling a small dictionary or even a grammar book for use on Jupiter.

Let me know your opinion of such a project.

Your pal

Irina


e-mail
Date: 26.1.2001     09.23.32
From: sio2c@allan.gla.sch.uk
To: iri2c@allan.jupiter.net

Dear Irina,

What you said in that last e-mail, I've got to know, was that for real? Did
you really mean I should just ask him if he wanted to get off with me?
And all that stuff about sexual congress, I don't know how to put this,
but, how far? You don't really mean all the way, do you? I suppose it must
be different on Jupiter but here you don't just go all the way with a boy,
well some folk do but everybody thinks they're slags and the boys don't
even like them after. I'm no like that. I mean, I'm no even 13 yet. And the
other thing is, well, that's no how I feel about him. I mean I fancy him, of
course I do, but it's more than that. I want to talk to him too and find out
more about him. I really really like him. And I don't know if he likes me
or not but he wouldn't if I just went up and asked him if he wanted to get
off with me. He's different, he's quiet.

Anyway the other stuff in your letter, I don't really understand what
you're on about. Are you saying that the way I talk is just as good as
proper English? Try telling Miss Macintosh that. I mean if you want tae
make up a Glaswegian dictionary, that's fine, it's a laugh. But it's no
right, is it?

But I still think Paul Wilson is more important. I hope you have time to e-mail me before Saturday, I really want to know what you think.

Your pal

Siobhan

e-mail
Date: 27.1.2001    02.45.67.43
From: iri2c@allan.jupiter.net
To: sio2c@allan.gla.sch.uk

Dear Siobhan,

I had no idea, even from our planetary files on human sociology, that your species was so undeveloped. I am most concerned that you should regard daydreaming about a male with whom you have had little contact as being of greater importance than linguistic concepts. I repeat that the way to conquer such an unhealthy obsession is to bring it out into the light of reality, and the quickest course is to approach this boy directly.

Your choice of words on this matter is interesting. 'To get off with' means, I presume, to have some preliminary physical contact, such as kissing. You then use phrases such as 'how far' and 'all the way'. Thus the sexual act is seen as some kind of route, which is mapped out in defined stages with a predicted end. This is unlike our view of a grouping of pleasurable experiences with less defined boundaries. Obviously, where the primary purpose of such an act is the production of offspring, this would, by necessity, involve what you describe as 'going all the way', but, as I have explained before, we Jupiterians rarely have the opportunity for such indulgence.

I hope you will not feel I have betrayed your confidence but I have confided in my mother about this matter, as she is something of an expert on the sociology of minor planets. She agrees with me about the unhealthiness of your fantasies but, with her greater experience, cautioned me to be judicious in my advice. While in a more advanced civilisation, the advice I gave you in my last letter would be correct, she feels that, under the circumstances in which you live, it would indeed be dangerous for you to overthrow your cultural norms in such an extreme way.

After reading your communications, she suggests that the main problem for you to conquer is your lack of self-worth. She notices that you seem to place excessive trust in the opinions of others (such as your teacher and, indeed, myself) and you hold a poor opinion of your own abilities, as demonstrated by your belief that this boy is superior to yourself; these attributes may stem from your feelings that your parents, especially your mother, prefer your brother. She says that there is nothing unusual in this for a female of your culture, though the absence of Scot-land from our statistical norms may mean that, in fact, you are even more prey to such self-deluding beliefs.

However, there are solutions to your difficulties. Should you have access to video-mail she could arrange a link with a suitably experienced programmer. Ten sessions of virtual therapy would delete all your negativity, while 20 would ascend you to a higher level of consciousness altogether, something approaching that of the average Jupiterian adolescent.

Even if this is not possible, there are some simple ways in which you can help yourself. She suggests that you start with a programme of positive belief reinforcements. Every hour you must tell yourself that you are, in fact, worthy and deserving of respect by repeating affirmations such as:

I am an intelligent, attractive and worthy individual.
I am in control of my emotions.
I am the author of my destiny.

You will find that even after a few days these will bring about improvements in your self-esteem. By Saturday you will not care whether or not Paul Wilson 'gets off with you'.

Your pal

Irina

e-mail
Date: 31.1.2001    2.43.34
From: sio2c@allan.gla.sch.uk
To: iri2c@allan.jupiter.net

Dear Irina,

I am an intelligent, attractive and worthy individual.
I am in control of my emotions.
I am the author of my destiny.

Tell your ma thanks very much for her help. The affirmations worked a treat but I'll no be needing the therapy. And I don't think you'll be hearing much from me again because I got off with Paul at the party and I think I'm gonnae be too busy for e-mails. Anyway it's been nice knowing you. Hope you get on OK with your dictionary.

Your pal,

Siobhan

# DEAR SANTA

Ma mammy disnae love me. Ah kin see it in her eyes, no the way she looks at me, but the way she looks through me, the way you look at sumpn that's been in the hoose fur years; you know it's there but you don't see it. It's hard no tae be seen, it makes you wee and crumpled up inside. When ah kiss her on the cheek, her skin creases, soft and squashy lik a marshmallow, and close up ah see the lines runnin doon the sidey her mooth and smell the powder on her face. She doesnae kiss me back.

*You kin read fur ten minutes but then that light's tae be aff.*

*Gonnae come and tuck me in, Mammy?*

*You're too big tae be tucked in.*

She keeps watchin the television.

*You tuck Katie in.*

*Katie's only five. You're a big girl.*

Ah'm eight year auld. Ah'm a big girl.

Ah don't know if ma mammy loved me afore Katie wis born, ah cannae mind that far back but ah must of been jealous when she was wee. Ah remember wan day she wis lyin sleepin in her pram ootside and ah got plastercine and made it intae wee balls and stuck them all ower her face; she looked as if she had some horrible disease. Ah mind staunin there lookin doon at that soft skin covered in sticky horrible purple lumps and felt good inside, warm and full.

43

Katie's asleep in the other bed, fair curly hair spread oot across the pillow, smilin in her sleep the way she does when she's awake. Ma sister is perfect, ah kin see that, she's wee and pretty and aye happy, bubblin ower wi life. When the sun shines, she's runnin aboot the gairden efter sunbeams and when it rains she pits on her wellies and splashes in the puddles. She never cries. Ma daddy says she's a princess, her teacher says she's an angel, ma mammy says,

*Why can't you be more like your sister?*

In the school nativity play Katie gets picked as the angel that tells Mary she's gonnae huv the baby Jesus so ma mammy sits up all night sewin her a white robe and a perra golden wings. Ah'm a shepherd, wi a stripy tea towel roon ma heid. In the photy she's at the front, in between Mary and Joseph, glitterin as if she really wis an angel, and ah'm this big lurkin thing at the endy the back row, daurk and blurred. The photy gets framed and put on the unit in the livin room.

*Thon's a lovely photy.*

*Katie's pure beautiful in that frock. She looks just lik an angel.*

*And Alison's gettin awful big fur her age.*

*Ah know, ah kin haurdly get anythin tae fit her. Ah hud tae pit panels intae her communion frock so she could wear it fur her confirmation and it's less than a year auld.*

It's Christmas Eve, the shops sparkle and we're in Debenham's queuein up tae see Santa. Ah don't think ah believe in Santa any mair but don't want tae admit it. Katie goes first and sits on his knee and tells him she wants a baby doll and a cot. Then she gies him a big kiss, slides doon fae his knee and runs towards ma daddy.

*Santa says if ah'm a good girl ah'll get it, Daddy.*

She pits her airms roon his neck and he birls her, wee legs stickin oot fae unner her frock.

*You're aye a good girl, princess.*

He smiles at me.

*On ye go, hen.*

Close up ah kin see Santa's beard is fake. The glue has dried on his skin and there's wee rolled-up rubbery bits on his cheek. But his knee feels solid tae sit on, and when he smiles the lines crinkle roon his blue eyes.

*And what's your name, pet?*

*Alison.*

*Whit age are you, Alison?*

*Eight.*

*You're a big girl for eight, aren't you? And whit dae you want for Christmas, Alison?*

Ah knew he wisnae Santa, no the real Santa that lives in Greenland wi the reindeer, if there is a real Santa anyway, but his eyes were kind and he called me by ma name and ah wanted to tell him, ah tried tae tell him.

*Ah want ma mammy tae . . .*

But then a big lump cam up, no in ma throat, but in ma hert, heavy and grey lik a stane, that stopped me fae sayin it.

*You want your mammy? Is she no here?*

He looked roon fur help as though he wis feart ah wis gonnae cry and he didnae want a greetin wean on his knee. Ah shook ma heid. He looked straight intae ma face.

*Whit dae you want fae Santa, Alison?*

*Ah don't know . . . ah know but ah cannae say.*

*Is it a secret?*

*Aye.*

*Ah tell you whit. Why don't you write it doon and . . . do you have a chimney at home?*

*No a real wan, it's a gas fire.*

*Well you put the letter in a secret place, and I'll find it. And if you're a good girl, you'll get what you want.*

Ah'm a good girl.

Christmas Eve ah'm sittin on the bed in ma pyjamas wi a pad of blue lined paper and a Biro. The room is daurk but the wee bedside lamp makes a white circle that lights up the page ah'm starin at. It's hard tae find the words.

*Dear Santa,*

*Please could you*

*I would like*

*If its no too much bother*

But what is it ah'm tryin tae say? Could you make ma mammy love me? That's no Santa's job, he's there tae gie oot sweeties and toys tae weans wanst a year, so there's nae point in askin him. If there is a Santa. Ah look oot the windae; the sky's dirty grey and ah don't think we'll huv a white Christmas somehow.

The door opens and ma mammy comes in. The hall light's on and her fair hair sticks oot all roon her heid, fuzzy and soft. A cannae see her face.

*Are you no asleep yet? It's nine o'clock.*

*Ah'm writin ma letter tae Santa.*

*Santa doesnae come if yer no sleepin. Look, there's Katie, sound.*

She bends ower Katie's bed, where she's lyin wi wan airm stickin oot fae under the covers. Ma mammy lifts the bedclothes ower her, then turns tae me.

*Hurry up and finish that letter, Alison. Ah'll pit it in fronty the fire and Santa'll get it when he comes.*

Ma mammy sits on the bed beside me while ah take a clean bit of paper and write dead slow so it's ma best writin.

*Dear Santa,*
*Please could i have a Barbie doll and a toy dog. I am a good girl.*
*Love*
*Alison*

Ah fold the paper twice, print SANTA on the front, then gie it tae ma mammy. She pits it in her pocket and lifts the covers fur me tae get inside. Ah coorie doon, watchin her hair glowin like a halo against the blackness of the room. Ah love strokin her hair, it's that soft and fuzzy but she cannae be bothered wi that and jerks her heid away, sayin *don't, you'll mess it up*, just lik she does when ma daddy tries tae touch it. But it's that quiet and still and she's in a good mood so ah lift ma haun and touch her hair, just a wee bit.

*Mammy, how come you've got fair hair and Katie's got fair hair and mines is broon?*

*You take efter yer daddy and Katie takes efter me.*

*Ah wisht ah had fair hair.*

*How? There's nothin wrang wi broon hair.*

*Ah wisht ah had hair lik yours.*

Ma mammy smiles and the lines roon her eyes get deeper but she looks at me mair soft like.

*Go tae sleep, hen, or Santa'll no come.*

She bends ower and kisses me, a dry kiss, barely grazin ma cheek, and before ah have time tae kiss her back she's switched off the bedside light, stood up and moved tae the door.

*Night, Alison.*

*Night, Mammy.*

She goes oot, nearly closin the door, but leavin a wee crack of light fallin across the bedclothes.

# WANNY THE LASSIES

Ah knew they were lyin right fae the start. We aw knew it, the lassies anyway. Ah couldnae unnerstaun how embdy could of took them seriously, been fooled by thae innocent looks, but then maisty the polis an teachers involved were men an it's amazin how men jist cannae believe that wee lassies a 14 can be bad, really bad. Daft an giggly, aye, but no the kinda badness that would make up sumpn lik that. Ah wonder whit the women teachers thoat.

*Anne Marie Connelly.*

Ah'm followin Miss McKenzie, the assistant heidie, doon the sterrs. She's a big wumman clickin alang in her peerie-heeled shoes an she wears this dead strong perfume, the kind that gets right in the backy yer throat, but it cannae disguise her ain smell, animal-like, as if you'd sprayed perfume ower a coo. She stauns wi her haun oan the door of the heidie's office an smiles at me.

*Now, I don't want you to get worried about this, Anne Marie. The police are questioning all the girls in your class; it's routine, you haven't done anything wrong. Just tell them the truth.*

Two big polis, a man and a wumman, are sittin there wi ma Guidance teacher, Wee Alec, a sweaty, specky man that twitches lik a dementit budgie if ye tell him ye've goat cramp. He cannae even look at you if he thinks it's anythin tae dae wi periods so the lassies are aye gaun tae him askin tae get sent hame. It's a wonder medical researchers huvnae descendit oan oor school demandin tae know why the female pupils of St Francis High huv periods oan average wanst a week.

The polisman stauns up, a big tumshie, his herr cut dead short so it shows aff the wrinkly bits behind his ears.

*Just sit down, Anne Marie.*

*Now there's nothing to worry about.*

Ah wisht everybdy wid stop tellin me there's nothin tae worry aboot.

*We just want to ask you a few questions. We just want you to tell us the truth.*

He sits doon in the chair opposite an draws it closer.

Ah nod ma heid.

*Right, Anne Marie, you know your Maths teacher, Mr Fletcher?*

*Aye.*

*Can you tell us what he's like in class, the way he behaves towards the pupils?*

Oh, so that's it.

*Well, he's a good laugh, he likes kiddin us oan. A mean we dae wer work tae, but . . .*

*I see. When you say he liked having a laugh, which pupils did he have a laugh with?*

*Well, Shuggie MacEvoy, he would kinda slag him aff a bit, kid him oan aboot his skinheid an that.*

*What about the girls in the class?*

He leans forward an pits his elbows oan his knees, claspin his hauns. Close up, his heid's even mair wrinkly an fulla lumps an bumps. We hud tae make a clay sculpture in Art wanst, an mines looked lik that, orangey-rid an covered in wrinkly bits an thumb marks ah couldnae smooth oot.

*Well, he used tae call us ladies an madam an aw that.*

*Did he single out any particular girls?*

*Well, some girls used tae hing aboot roon him.*

*June Ritchie and Maria Saunders — would you say they were particular favourites of Mr Fletcher?*

*Ah widnae say favourites, Ah mean, he wis nice tae us aw, but they sat at the fronty the class an they used tae talk tae him a lot.*

*Do you remember Mr Fletcher saying, 'You're so beautiful, June, I wish I was on a desert island with you?'*

*Ah don't know.*

*Or 'You shouldn't wear skirts like that to school if you expect me to concentrate on my work.'*

*Ah never heard him.*

*Other girls in the class heard him.*

*Well, ah sit at the backy the class.*

Ah dae noo but ah didnae at the starty the year. Isobel an me sat in the front seats, no because we're swots or that but because we were last inty the room an they were the only two seats left apart fae the wans in fronty Wullie Hughes an Jimmy Rose, an you widnae sit in fronty them unless ye were needin yer heid looked. They spend aw their time pokin ye wi rulers an makin filthy remarks.

*Seeza feely yer tits, darlin.*

*Whit colour knickers you goat oan the day?*

*Bet she disny wear any knickers.*

Anyway ah don't mind sittin at the front because ah want tae dae well at school. Ah widnae say that tae emdy cos they jist call you a swot, so ye huvtae moan aboot how much ye hate school or naebdy wid speak tae ye, but ah don't hate it. Ah'm no genius but ah can dae OK in maist subjects if ah listen an dae ma hamework, an ah want tae get a good job when ah leave school, in an office, or maybe even go tae college or that. Ah don't want tae end up lik ma big sister Jean, workin in the baker's cos she spent her time at school havin a laugh an paintin her nails at the backy the room.

An when it turnt oot that oor new Maths teacher wis a good-lookin young guy the lassies aw wisht they'd sat at the fronty the room. Though Mr Fletcher wisnae that good lookin, tae be honest. He wis quite small for a man, wi pale blue eyes an wavy broon herr he kept pushin back oot his face, but he wis a right laugh, aye pullin yer leg, an when he smiled ye felt warm inside. An a young man teacher disnae need tae be Brad Pitt for the lassies tae fancy him. There's no that much talent nickin aboot schools. After aw, if teachers were that good-lookin they'd be models or pop stars insteidy teachers, wouldn't they? We startit tae look forward tae Maths. An efter aboot a week June and Maria came up tae me an Isobel at playtime.

*How d'yous fancy swoppin seats wi us in the Maths class?*

June's smilin as if we were her best pals. She has big, very white teeth and her lips are carefully outlined in sweety-pink lipstick.

*How?*

Ah'm no bein nasty or that, just no smilin back.

*Maria's eyesight isnae that good. She cannae see the board fae where we're sittin.*

*Why doesn't she wear her glasses then?*

Ah look at Maria, a big skinny dreepy a lassie that never hus anythin tae say fur herself, jist relies on June tae dae aw the talkin. Which is nae hardship tae June. Maria pushes her long dark herr away fae her face.

*Ah've loast them. Ma mammy's gonnae get me contacts when ma da comes hame fae the rigs.*

June keeps smilin at us, but she's staunin too close tae me noo an ah can smell the conditioner in her herr an see the blobs a black where her mascara's caked too thick.

*So ye see, we need tae sit at the front mair than yous dae.*

Her airm's pressin against me noo, nudgin me slightly, pushin me close tae the cauld brick wa. Ah look at Isobel who has her eyes turnt doon tae the grund.

*Aye. Aw right.*

A thoat it wid be lik *LA Law*, Ah suppose evrybdy dis, aw sharp incisive cut an thrusts:

*I put it to you that at 7.32 pm on the evening of the 24th of September you were seen leaving the house of the deceased, carrying a blood-stained kitchen knife.*

Then they produce a witness who jist happened to be usin her binoculars at 7.32 pm an you think that's it, till the defence produce evidence that her clock wis an hour fast, an you think he's got off, then forensic find the blood-stained shirt cuff, provin that only a person of the rare blood group Z (jist discovered 15 minutes before in a laboratory in Hong Kong but tested via the Internet . . .) could huv committed the murder.

Shite.

The furst thing ah noticed aboot the court wis how shabby it wis. The fancy poalished widden seats look scuffed an sad close up, empty rows lik a church at a funeral a somebody unloved. An as for the lawyers, nervous wee sweetie-wives ye widnae trust wi a bagga jelly babies, never mind yer defence oan a charge lik that.

Aw except the main man fur the prosecution; he wis the goods, tall wi a deep voice an a crisp clear way a speakin, his words ringin oot lik footsteps oan a silent frosty night.

*And do you think these remarks were appropriate for a male teacher to say to his young female pupils?*

*But he didnae say them seriously, he wis jist kiddin on like.*

He turns an takes five steps away fae me, puttin his feet down sole-first, quiet, cat-like. Then suddenly he birls roon tae face me.

*And did Mr Fletcher ever touch any of the girls?*

He emphasises the word *touch*, spittin oot the *ti* an *chi* sounds as if he wis givin elocution lessons.

*No really.*

*What do you mean by that? Either he touched them or he didn't.*

*No the way you're meanin. He sometimes put his airm roon you or that but it wis jist furra laugh.*

He raises his eyebrows so they looked lik an upturned V.

*So he did sometimes touch girls?*

*Aye.*

*Pardon?*

*Yes.*

*Did you see him putting his arm round June?*

*Yes.*

It's funny bein a witness in the coort. Ah mean, you'd think bein a witness wid mean they wanted you tae tell them everythin that you witnessed, exactly how it happened, but it's no like that. The way they ask the questions ye cannae explain things, so it comes oot aw distortit, it disnae feel right whit you're sayin, lik the way yer face feels when ye've hud a jag at the dentist an cannae drink oot wan sidey yer mooth. Ye've no tellt a lie but ye huvny tellt the truth either. An the way thon lawyer spoke, it wis as if Mr Fletcher wis a filthy pervert an June an Maria were two innocent wee lassies whose only interest in him wis findin oot how tae solve a quadratic equation. Ah wisht he'd been there, in the classroom.

*Sur, are you merrit?*

June sittin oan tappy her desk wi her legs crossed. You can see her knickers. Maria sittin behind her, combin oot June's blonde hair.

*I am indeed, June.*

*Are ye happily merrit, sur?*

*Yes June, very.*

*Does yer wife satisfy ye, sur?*

The resty the class are gigglin noo, embarrassed, but enjoyin the show. June turns roon, showin aff even mair leg in the process.

*Ah didnae mean that, ya shower a durty busturds — aw ah'm sorry, sur, it jist slipped oot — ah mean, is yer wife a good cook, sur? Does she keep ye satisfied wi yer meals?*

*Yes, June, my wife is a very good cook. Now, d'you think you could sit in your seat and open your jotter for me?*

*That's no all she'll open fur ye.*

*William Hughes, did you say something?*

*Ah said, d'ye want me tae open the windae fur ye?*

*No, thank you, William. Let's get on with our work.*

Ah could never quite figure oot whether Mr Fletcher wis a bit daft, or jist too saft fur his ain good. He must of known June wis totally ooty order but he never tried tae stop her. Well, that's no completely true, he did at times but it wis aye too late. Some teachers are like that — it's as if they've nae sense a timin. Folk that are skilled at sumpn, whether it's footie or ironin — they huv this inbuilt sense that tells them when tae go wi the flow an when tae haud back. An watchin them dae whitever it is they dae well, whether it's Ronaldo puttin thon ball intae the net or ma granny smoothin her iron intae the creases at the seam of a blouse, yer filled wi the rhythm an rightness a whit they're daein. It's like that wi teachers, the good wans, no the jist-good-enoughs. They know when tae take a joke an when tae nip wan in the bud, when tae work ye right hard an when tae ease up, which pupils tae encourage an which tae sit oan. There's a sense a purpose in their classes. An fur aw that we liked Mr Fletcher an he wis nice an quite good at explainin things on the board, he didnae huv it — fur he let June an Maria go too far.

*Were you aware that June and Maria had been babysitting for Mr Fletcher?*

*Oh aye, we aw knew that.*

*Did they speak about their experiences?*

Did they speak aboot it? Did they ever shut up aboot it? Whit wis he playin at, though, askin the perry them tae babysit? Did he think if they saw his baby an his wife an his hoose, they'd realise he widnae be interested in daft lassies like them, or mibby if he made them feel special, they'd stop showin aff an talkin durty in class? Ah don't know, but whitever it wis, it didnae work. The first time they tellt us aboot it as if they'd been fur tea wi the Queen. There wis a huddle a lassies roon them at the starty every period an at playtime an lunchtime, drinkin in the details.

*Two patterns a wallpaper an matchin borders.*

*Kinda peachy-colour.*

*Keeps his drink in a cabinet under the TV.*

*Whisky, Jack Daniels.*

*She must drink vodka.*

*Her name's Magret, she's nice, but.*

*Left us tea on a tray, an ginger biscuits fae Marks.*

*Ran us hame efter in his motor.*

They startit babysittin every Friday night for the Fletchers, so they could go tae the pictures or sometimes fur a meal. An June an Maria did calm doon a bit in class, there wis less durty talk, but they startit hingin roon him as if he wis their personal property. It would huv gied ye the dry boak tae hear them sookin up tae him, aw sweetie-sweetie.

*How's David's cold the day, sir?*

*He's a lot better, thanks.*

*We were affa worried aboot him when he startit coughin on Friday. If you hudnae come back then we'd huv phoned the doctor.*

*You're very sensible, June, I'm glad I can rely on you.*

She turns an looks at the resty us wi a smarmy smile oan her face.

*At some point in January this year, June and Maria stopped babysitting for Mr Fletcher. Do you know why?*

It wis a week later we fun oot whit hud happened. Wan Monday mornin Mary McKenzie comes intae registration an stops at June's desk. She's a hefty lassie wi chunky thighs, brilliant at hockey. She's no good-lookin exactly but she has clear pinky skin an shiny straight thick hair, an Wullie Hughes groans oot loud an sticks his chist oot lik a doo oan heat when she walks past him. No that she'd huv any time fur an eejit lik him.

*Ma cousin Lorraine was babysittin fur Mr Fletcher on Friday.*

June looks up fae her magazine.

*Oh, aye.*

In the fluorescent light her skin's lik the left-ower dauds a dough yer mammy used tae let ye play wi when she'd been bakin an apple tart.

Agnes Mitchell, her ferrety wee face turnin roon fae the seat in front, beady eyes bright as comets.

*A thoat that wis your job, June, you an Maria.*

*We've given it up – better things tae dae on a Friday night than look after a screamin wean.*

Mary stauns beside June's desk, lookin doon at her.

*Lorraine says he gave you the sack. Mr Fletcher tellt her yous got pissed on his drink wan night. His wife said you werenae fit tae look efter a wean.*

June's mooth purses up, the sweetie-pink lipstick smudgin in the creases. She lifts her magazine tae her face.

A suppose we underestimated June, us lassies. We were that chuffed aboot her gettin her comeuppance and we thoat she'd huv the sense tae keep her trap shut fae noo on aboot Mr Fletcher.

*Right, I'd like to hear some of the short stories you were writing for homework. Would anyone like to volunteer to read theirs out loud to the class?*

Miss McTear looks roon eagerly. She's aye eager, noddin her wee heid lik a noddin dug in the backy a motor.

*Ah'll dae mines.*

June's voice rises fae the backy the room, skraikin lik a craw that's hud too many fags. Miss McTear hesitates fur a moment, obviously surprised at a lazy cow lik June volunteerin fur anythin, but then starts noddin her heid up an doon, her roon glasses glintin.

*Oh well done, June, let's hear it. Title?*

*Huvnae goat wan yet.*

*Oh, right, well, maybe we can help you with that later. Do you want to stand up so we can hear you better?*

*Can ah come oot tae the front an sit oan yer desk?*

*Oh, right, yes, of course, June.*

Miss McTear waves June tae the teacher's desk an sits in the second row, jist in fronty me an Isobel, her heid still noddin. June starts readin her story, slow an deliberate, pronouncin every word like a wean learnin tae read.

*The bedroom was painted pale blue with a border of wee blue flowers round the ceiling. As he led me into it, I could smell the scent of his Lynx aftershave. There was a huge kingsized bed with a dark blue downie cover on it. He led me to it and we sat down.*

*Would you like a glass of champagne, darling? he said in my ear.*

*There was already a bottle and two glasses waiting on the pine bedside table.*

*Well, all right, I replied.*

*He poured it into the glasses and we started to drink.*

*I just can't help myself, I'm madly in love with you, he said hoarsely.*

*He started to kiss me passionately on the lips.*

*But what about your wife? I replied.*

*She does not satisfy me any more, since the baby she has lost her desires for me, if you know what I mean.*

*He put his hand on my breast and I could feel his hot breath on my neck.*

*I love you, I want to marry you as soon as you are 16. I will get a divorce, darling.*

*He was on top of me by this time. I tried to struggle but he kept kissing me and I was overcome, I think I almost passed out. He kept kissing me as his hands pulled off my clothes, ripping my tights and my knickers in his haste.*

*I want you, I need you, be mine, he moaned.*

*I could not hold back any longer. I surrendered myself to him.*


Silence so thick it was as if a fog had rolled doon ower the room an you couldny see anybdy else. A wee giggle, jist a squeak, a whimper, and another silence. Then Wullie Hughes lets oot a huge loud fart an the class falls aboot laughin. Miss McTear twitchin an shakin, hauf-in hauf-oot her seat, no knowin whether tae tackle Wullie or June furst.

*Now, calm down, calm down. Willie Hughes . . .*

*It's Wullie, no Willie . . . an ah couldnae help it, miss.*

*You'll have to learn to control yourself.*

*Ma da says better oot than in.*

*Your da's not in the room just now . . . June, you may sit down.*

*Ur ye no gonnae tell me whit ye thinky ma story, miss?*

*Later, June, I'll discuss it in detail with you. I think you should read less bestsellers though, if you want to write well. Write from your own experience.*

*But ah jist did.*

Silence again, everybdy watchin June an Miss McTear, lookin at each other across the room, lik gunfighters in an auld cowboy film.

*Don't talk nonsense, June. There's the bell, pack up now.*

We never fund oot who reportit June's story tae wee Alec. It wisnae Miss McTear, she's no that daft, an it wisnae June either. Ah don't think she wanted tae get hersel involved wi the polis, jist tae embarrass him an make hersel look big. Some folk said he got an anonymous phone call. Or mibby it wisnae anyone in particular, jist a rumour, sneakin roon the school lik a bad smell, that made him question June an she couldnae bring hersel tae back doon. Mibby.

Or it could've been sumbdy jealous of June, of all that attention she got, wanny the lassies that wantit tae babysit fur Mr Fletcher, tae sit in his hoose drinkin tea an eatin ginger biscuits, watchin his TV while his wean wis sleepin sound in the next room, every now an then gaun tae check on him. Till they come back fae the pictures an he runs her hame in his motor, her sittin close tae him in the darkness, watchin the windscreen wipers sweepin through the shinin drops a rain.

# A CHITTERIN BITE

We'd go tae the baths every Saturday mornin, Agnes and me. Ah'd watch fae the windae, alang the grey, gluthery street, till ah caught the first glimpse of her red raincoat and blue pixie hat turnin the corner, then ah'd grab ma cossie, wrap it up in the blue-grey towel, washed too many times, and heid for the door.

*Ah'm away, Mammy.*

Ma mammy would appear fae the kitchen, haudin a wee bundle, wrapped up in the waxed paper fae the end of the loaf.

*Here you are, hen, your chitterin bite.*

Inside were two jammy pieces, wan for me and wan for Agnes, tae eat efter the swimmin on the way alang the road, a chitterin bite, no enough tae fill your belly, just somethin tae stave aff the chitterin cauld when you come oot the baths.

The noise hits you the minute you open that big green door; the ceilin high and pointy like a chapel roof, makin everythin echo roon its beams. It leaks, so drips of watter plash on your heid while you're swimmin. The place is fulla weans, screechin at their pals ower the racket. Two boys are leppin in fae the side till big Alex blaws his whistle and threatens tae pap them oot. There's a row a boxes at each side of the pool, the hauf-doors painted bright blue, the left-haun side for the women and the right fur the men. Agnes and me get changed in the wan cubicle; her cossie has blue ruched bits aw roon, while mines is yella wi pink flooers. You can just see the two wee bumps startin tae grow on her chist and she footers aboot, sortin her straps tae try tae cover them.

*Whit dae they feel like?*

*You can touch them if you want.*

Ah push two fingers gently intae her left breist which goes in a wee bit under the pressure.

*Is it sore?*

*Naw, disnae feel like anythin really.*

Ah look doon at ma ain chist, totally flat. Ma mammy says ah'll be next but ah cannae imagine it.

*C'mon, let's get a move on, ah'm freezin.*

We run oot the cubicle and plunk straight intae the watter, the shock of the cauld makin us scream as usual. Ah hate jumpin intae the baths but ah love it as well.


I still go swimming, but now to the warm and brightly lit leisure centre with its saunas and steam rooms, aromatherapy massages and hot showers. Tuesday is Ladies' Night and I drive there in my car; shampoo, conditioner and body lotion tucked neatly in my designer sportsbag along with a change of clothing. Dressed-up clothing; short skirt, sheer tights and silky shirt.

Afterwards I meet Matthew in the Italian restaurant, an anonymous place tucked away in a side street. We are unlikely to be spotted here, for there are several places with cheaper food and more atmosphere in the area, so Matthew and I have made it our own. As I push open the door I see he is sitting at our usual table, his head bent over the menu, dark shiny hair neatly slicked back with gel. He looks up as I cross the room and I feel my breath catch in my throat.

He goes to the gym on Tuesdays before he comes to meet me so we're both showered, powdered and squeaky-clean. I breathe in the sweet scent of his aftershave and the clean soapy smells of his body. His lips graze my cheek but I am aware that his eyes scan the room, just in case anyone is watching. I sit opposite him, feeling the thick white tablecloth under my hands, knowing we both look good in the pinkish glow of the candlelight. I finger the heavy wine glass, rolling the stem between my thumb and index finger, sipping delicately.

The cauld hits you as soon as you're ootside, efter the heavy door sclaffs shut. Oor hair is soakin, plastered tae wer heids, and wee dreeps run doon the back of yer neck. Ma mammy says put your pixie on efter the swimmin or you'll get a cauld in the heid, but that just makes it worse, the damp seeps through tae you feel your brain's frozen up inside. Agnes and me walk, airms linked, stuffin dauds a breid intae wer mooths. Ma mammy saves us the big thick enders that you sink yer teeth intae, the raspberry jam runnin oot and tricklin doon yer chin. Ah wipe it away wi the endy the damp towel.

The café is two streets away. The windaes are aye steamed up so you cannae see in and the name, 'Bellini's', is printed above the door in fancy red letters. As you push open the heavy doors, heat whaps you that hard it's like bein slapped roon the face, and yer heid starts tae tingle. The café is divided up intae booths, each wi gless panels, frosted like sugar icing, so when you're inside it you feel you're in yer ain wee world. The seats flip up and doon on creaky metal hinges and you have tae watch or you catch yer fingers in them. No that Agnes and me sit in the booths very often. We hardly ever have enough money for a sit-in. Usually we just get a cone or a bag of sweeties. But in the winter the smell of chips and the steam risin fae the frothy coffee makes your belly feel that empty.

Agnes and me pool wer money, leavin aside what we need tae get intae the pictures.

*What'll we get – midget gems?*

*We got them last week – whit aboot cherry lips?*

*Aye, quarter a cherry lips, please.*

Cherry lips are ma favourites: they're harder than midget gems but wi a funny taste tae them, wersh almost, no like any other sweeties. But the best thing is their shape; they're like wee smiley mooths aboot an inch wide an if you sook in yer ain lips and stick a cherry wan on tap it looks dead funny. Sometimes me n Agnes dae that an kid on we're kissin, just like at the pictures. Agnes crosses her eyes and makes me laugh and the cherry lips fall oot.

Affairs have their own rules, unspoken, unwritten, which soon become engraved on your heart.

1. Never go anywhere you are likely to be seen together.
2. Never show affection in public.
3. Never mention his wife.
4. Never cry.
5. Never phone him at home.
6. Never give your name if you phone him at work.
7. Never whinge if he has to cancel a meeting.
8. Never tell your friends about him.
9. Never leave marks on him.

It would be more satisfying if there were ten rules but I can't think of another.

I just broke the last rule. I can see the purply-red mark, about an inch across, nestling just above his left shoulder blade, where he won't see it, but she will. I didn't do it deliberately, but what does that mean? I knew I was sooking a wee bit harder than I usually do, for a wee bit longer, yes. I wasn't really sinking my teeth into him with force, I couldn't tell it was going to leave a mark, not for sure. Guilty or not guilty? I lean, propped up on my elbow, and watch him, sleeping, lying on his right side, dark whispers of hair fanning across white sheets, like an ad for some expensive perfume. Soon he will wake and I will watch him putting on his clothes, which now lie neatly folded over the chair, he will kiss me without looking into my eyes and I will close the door on him and stand, listening as his footsteps echo down the hallway.

We go tae the pictures every week efter the swimmin, scramblin tae get the chummy seats up the back, sharin wer sweeties, grabbin each other's airms at the scary bits and gigglin at the love scenes. Then wan week, when we're walkin alang the road efter the baths, Agnes says:

*Ah said we'd meet Jimmy McKeown and his pal at the pictures.*

*What?*

*He wants tae go wi me. He says he'll bring his pal for you.*

*Do you want tae go wi him?*

*Ah don't know, ah'll gie it a try.*

Ah unlinked ma airm fae Agnes's and marched on, starin ahead.

*Well, you don't need me tae come too.*

Agnes caught up wi me, grabbin at ma airm.

*Ah cannae go masel.*

*How no?*

*Ah just cannae. Anyway, he's bringin his pal. If you don't go, ah canae go. Come on, Mary, be a pal.*

The boys are waitin for us inside the foyer of the picture hoose. Jimmy McKeown is a year aulder than us, wi a broad nose, a bit bent tae the side, and straight dirty-fair hair in a side shed. The pal is staunin hauf behind him, a wee skinny laddie wi roond baby cheeks and red lips like a lassie.

*This is Shuggie, he's ma cousin.*

*This is Mary.*

*Hiya.*

*Will we go in?*

*After yous, girls.*

They're polite, even though Jimmy is actin the big shot and the pal still hasnae opened his mooth. Agnes and me go first, intae the daurk picture hoose, Agnes leadin the way tae the back row where the chummy seats are. She sits doon in wan but when ah go tae sit next tae her she mutters *naw, you huvtae sit wi Shuggie* and shoves me ower tae the next seat, where the airm rest forms a barrier between me and her. Ah feel Shuggie's knees pushin intae mines as he squeezes by me tae sit in the other hauf of the seat. Ah move as far ower tae the side nearest Agnes as ah can, but ah cannae help smellin the rough hairy smell of his sports jaicket under the sourness of the aftershave he must of plastered on his baby cheeks.

I don't expect the phone call. Not so soon anyway, not at work, not at ten o'clock in the morning, sitting at my bright shiny desk with my red folder in front of me and my bright shiny, perfectly modulated work voice;

*Good morning, Mary Henderson speaking, how may I help you?*

*Mary? It's me, Matthew, listen, I've got to talk to you, it's urgent. Can you meet me for lunch?*

*Of course.*

*Look, I can't talk now. Can you meet me in Sarti's? One o'clock?*

*OK. Make it quarter to, though, you know how busy it gets there.*

*Right. See you then.*

*

At lunchtime Sarti's is full of people in suits from nearby offices and the atmosphere is warm and faintly smoky. We sit down at a table just opposite the deli counter, which is piled high with different kinds of *panettone*. Matthew looks immaculate in his grey suit and silk floral tie but, as he bends his head to look at the menu, I notice a few stray bristly hairs, just where his cheekbone joins his neck, which he must have missed when shaving this morning. He looks at the menu as he speaks.

*What are you having?*

*Spaghetti vongole, I think. I'm starving. Maybe a night of passion makes you hungry.*

He looks up but does not smile.

*I don't have time for lunch. I think I'll just have coffee and a bit of cake.*

*A chitterin bite.*

*What?*

*It's what we used to call a bite to eat, not a full meal, just enough to keep the cold out after the swimming.*

He folds the menu up and replaced it in its holder.

*Speaking of bites . . .*

I look him straight in the eyes.

*Mary, do you know what kind of a mark you left on me last night?*

*Did I?*

He squeezes his left hand tight into a fist, then releases it, repeating the movement several times as though it were an exercise.

*She went berserk when she saw it.*

*What did you tell her?*

*I must have bruised myself at the gym, crap like that. How the hell do you bruise yourself on the shoulder blade? I'm sure she doesn't believe me but I think she's accepted it.*

*That's good.*

*For heaven's sake, couldn't you be more careful?*

*Must have been carried away by passion, I suppose.*

*You don't seem to be all that concerned about it.*

*I'm not the one that's cheating on my wife.*


We never spoke aboot it, Agnes and me, though, as the week progressed, a cauldness grew between us, a damp seepin cauld like the wan that gets intae your bones when you don't dry yourself quick enough efter the swimmin. And the next Saturday, when ah haunded her her piece and jam, she shook her heid and looked away fae me.

*Naw thanks, Mary, ah said ah'd meet Jimmy at Bellini's and we're gonnae have chips.*

*Oh.*

She put her airm in mines.

*You can come too. It'll be good tae get sumpn hot inside us steidy just a chitterin bite. We'll go tae the pictures efter. Shuggie's no gonnae be there, it's OK.*

Ah pulled ma airm free of Agnes's.

*Two's company, three's a crowd. Ah'll see you at school on Monday.*

The sky was heavy and grey and fulla rain. Ah didnae want tae go hame but ah couldnae think of where else tae go so ah wandered roon the streets, gettin mair and mair droukit, no really payin any heed tae where ah was goin, till ah fund masel ootside Bellini's. Ah cooried doon in a close on the other side of the street and watched the door till ah seen them come oot. Agnes was laughin as Jimmy held the door open for her. Their faces were pink wi the heat and Agnes's hair had dried noo, intae wee fuzzy curls aw ower her heid. They set aff towards the pictures, him cairryin her towel under his airm. Ah unwrapped ma piece and took a bite. The breid was hard and doughy and, as ah chewed, it didnae seem tae saften, so the big lumps stuck in ma throat. Ah stood up and heided for hame. As ah passed the waste grund on the corner, ah flung the pieces tae the birds.

*I'm sorry, Mary, I think it would be better if we didn't see each other for a while.*

*A while?*

*She's going to be suspicious. She'll be watching my every move at the moment. If we wait a few weeks she'll calm down and then we can go back to where we were.*

*Which is?*

*I thought we both knew the score.*

How could I have fallen in love with someone who used expressions like that, like something out of a bad film. But I had.

*Mary, you know I love you, I really do, but I can't leave her and the kids. I've never pretended I could. What we have together is very precious to me, but if it's not enough for you . . .*

Someone opened the door behind us and a cold draught cut through the heat of the restaurant. I looked across at Matthew, so beautiful in his perfect suit, and shook my head.

*No, it's not enough. You're right. We have to end it.*

*I'm sorry.*

*So am I.*

The waitress arrived with Matthew's coffee and piece of *panettone*. He looked at it for a moment, then at me.

*Look, I'm sorry, I don't think I can face this. Do you mind?*

*No, it's OK, on you go.*

He reached across the table and held my hand, squeezing it gently.

*Look after yourself.*

*You too.*

*Look, I really am sorry, I just can't talk just now.*

*It's OK. Just go, I'll be fine.*

He stood up and walked past me, brushing against my shoulder on the way out. I stared at the empty seat in front of me.

*Spaghetti vongole?*

*Thank you.*

*Black pepper? And Parmesan?*

She flourished the pepper mill, spooned Parmesan over the dish, then left.

Steam rose from the spaghetti and the clam shells gleamed dully like slate roof tiles. It smelled wonderful and I was starving. I picked up my fork, twirled the pasta round and round, pressing it against the spoon, and ate.

# ME AND THE BABBIE

*Och, look at his wee feet!*
*Och, look at his wee toes!*
*Och, look at his wee ears!*

Three week auld, lyin there in his simmit, eyes startin tae loss their bright baby blue, still there roon the edges but the centre turnin dark, like me, no his daddy. Wee Muppety hauns flailin aboot, but he kicked his heels wi determination, for aw the world as if he wis settin off on a march.

*Is he a good baby?*

Whit did they mean? How can a baby be good? Or bad? Whit they really mean is, does he sleep?

Naw, he never slept, no in his cot or his pram or any of the places he wis supposed tae sleep onyway. He slept on the breist, in ma airms, on ma lap, but the second ah tried tae pit him doon he opened his eyes, jerked his body as if he wis havin a fit, and started bawlin his heid aff.

Ma mammy said *stoap cuddlin him, you're makin a rod for yer back.*

Ma daddy said *he's exercisin his lungs.*

Ma sister said *pit him in his cot and leave him tae greet.*

Then there wis the feedin. He seemed tae want it 24 hour a day. He sooked and he sooked and hauf the time ah couldnae tell if he wis asleep or awake but if ah tried tae take him aff he bawled that much ah'd have tae pit him back on. And ah could hardly find time tae get tae the toilet,

let alane get washed or get sumpn tae eat, and ah certainly couldnae dae ony hoosework or make ma man's dinner.

Ma ma said *gie him ten minutes each side then take him aff*.

And ma da said *gie him a dummy*.

And ma sister said *pit him oan the bottle*.

And ah felt in ma hert they were wrang but ah didnae know whit wis right. And ah wis knackered and confused and sick of the whole lot ae them. Then he got fed up wi the hoose lookin like a tip and the wean aye feedin or girnin, and he wanted his tea on the table and me in his bed. Wan day he just packed his stuff and buggered aff.

*Ah'm no ready fur this*, he said.

And that was us, me and the babbie, ten flair up, birdseye view of the city night.

Ma mammy said *come and stay wi us*.

Ma daddy said *ah never liked him onyway*.

Ma sister said *could you no have been mair careful?*

And ah said *go away and leave me alane*. They went aff in a huff and ah looked at him and thought, this is it, there's just me and the babbie.

So ah stopped worryin aboot whit they thought.

And ah fed him aw night, takin him intae the bed wi me, where ah could feel his warm wee body and his soft airms and hear him breathin in the night. Ah didnae know how many feeds he'd had, cos he fell asleep and ah fell asleep and when ah woke up sometimes he'd be sleepin and sometimes sookin.

And in the morn he'd lie on the bed, kickin his wee legs and us cooried doon thegether, me talkin and him starin, then, as he got bigger, smilin, then makin cooin noises. Ah decided that ah widnae put him doon if he didny like it, so ah bought wanny they baby slings second haun, and just got by wi what ah could dae cairryin him aboot, makin a cuppa tea or washin the odd dish. Ah'd haurdly ony dishes tae wash since he left. Ah just used the wan plate, eatin wi the fork in wan haun and him in the ither, lived on pasta, so ah did, sick of the sight ae it, but he wis happy.

And in the mornins, we walked aboot, sometimes intae toon if it wis rainin, but maistly tae the park, me tellin him aboot the daffodils comin oot and the leaves on the trees. Ah'd have tellt him mair aboot the flooers and the trees but ah never knew their names. Ah'd take pieces wi me and eat them in the park, sittin on a bench. Ah fed him as well, wrapped up in a shawl wi ma jaicket roon me so naebdy could see whit ah wis daein. We stayed oot as long as we could so's no tae run up the heatin bills – the flat's all eletric and it's dear. At night we wrapped up warm thegither in bed and ah watched TV and fed him and he dozed and fed till ah pit oot the light, then he fed and slept till the morn.

And wan day wis much like another. Sometimes ah wis bored or tired or desperate for a cuppa tea and ah could of wept. Sometimes ah did have a wee greet, on ma ain, at night. But ah'd decided tae dae whitever it wis that would keep him happy, however strange it seemed tae other folk. For whit else wis there but me and the babbie. And he wis happy, hardly grat. But they couldnae leave me alane.

Ma mammy said *it's no natural, the way thon wean gets treated.*

Ma daddy said *he should be sleepin in his ain cot.*

Ma sister said *you need a night oot, ah'll babysit fur ye.*

A night oot – daein whit? Gaun tae the dancin wi a pack a daft lassies?

*No thanks, ah don't want tae leave him while ah'm still feedin him.*

Ma mammy said *it'll no hurt him tae take a bottle for wanst.*

Ma daddy said *he should be wi other folk sometimes.*

Ma sister said *he'll grow up tae be a right wee mammy's boy the way you're gaun on.*

But there wis naethin they could dae. The babbie wis healthy and happy and kept on growin and growin, fat wee face like an auld man, soft chubby legs, skin that made ma ain hauns feel like roughcast agin him. Ah wonder how babies can bear tae let us touch them.

There wis wan thing that bothered me though, and ah knew it wis daft but it kept nigglin away, gnawin at me so it grew and grew the way daft things sometimes become mair important than the big wans. Wi him gone there wis nae money, and though ah could stay oot aw day and go tae bed tae save the heatin, and the faimly allowance just aboot covered the nappies, ah'd nae money for claes fur him. Ma sister's wean wis six month aulder than him and she passed stuff on tae me and at first ah didnae care fur he was aye needin changed, and wan Babygro looks much like anither. But as he got aulder and mair of a wee person, ah got sick of the haund-me-doons.

Ah wantit the babbie tae wear green and lilac and even pink, the colours of the spring that wis all roon us. Ah wanted him tae have flooers or a bunny on his claes. Ah knew they'd aw think ah wis tryin tae turn him intae a wee lassie but that's no it. It wis just, ah don't know, but it wis comin up Easter Sunday and every Easter when ah wis wee ah used tae get a new ootfit; hat, gloves, frock for gaun tae the chapel. And ah wanted him tae have sumpn new, his ain, that ah'd picked for him, in colours that suited his skin and his eyes and his nature.

On the Saturday afore Easter it poured wi rain. Ah went tae the St Enoch Centre tae keep dry and, while ah wis in Debenham's, ah seen them, they were beautiful — lilac dungarees and a pale green top.

*Whit do you think, babbie? Do you like them?*

And he smiled and his wee legs kicked as if tae say *aye*.

So ah knocked them.

Ah don't know how ah managed it but there wis naebdy aboot so ah wheeched them intae his pram under the covers and left, pushin the pram casually, lookin roon at the displays as ah went. Aw through the shop ah expected a big haun on ma shouder, and even walkin alang the street ah didnae feel safe for ah've heard they let you leave the shop afore they nab you. But ah walked and ah walked, then eventually slowed doon when ah knew ah wis safe.

And the babbie looked perfect on Easter Sunday.

And ah know ah should of been thankful that ah'd no been caught and left it at that, but of course ah didnae. Ah'd never knocked anythin in ma life, never even thought aboot it, but wanst ah'd got away with it, it startit tae niggle at me like an itch. Ah'd find masel walkin through shops and seein sumpn ah liked, maybe feelin it wi ma haun, almost liftin it, edgin it a few inches towards ma bag. It wisnae conscious, it wis as if ma body wis daein it by itsel wioot ma say-so. It scared me and ah decided ah'd stop gaun intae toon so's tae keep oot of temptation's way.

Then ah got the next lot ae claes fae ma sister. And they were grey. Wee tracksuit tops and breeks in grey wi a navy or rid stripe on them. Grey for the babbie wi his peachy skin and his big hazel eyes. Sports claes for a four-month-auld. Ah hate grey. Why should he have tae wear grey because ah've nae money?

But this time of course ah got caught. And ah think how could ah have been so stupit, how could ah have risked everythin for that, but it's too late. You don't think, when you're daein sumpn, it happens too fast. It's only efter that you know whit's important and whit isnae.

The lawyer says ah'll get aff, no way would they put me away, first offence, young baby, extenuating circumstances. But whit if the lawyer's wrang, ah heard there are loads of women in jail just cos they've no paid their TV licence. And if me and the babbie werenae thegither, if they took him away fae me, ah don't think ah could bear it.

# AWAY IN A MANGER

Amy's haund was roastin in they furry mitts, felt like a wee mouse or a hamster in Sandra's palm; heat seepin through, warmin her. They turned off of Argyle Street intae the long dark road, Amy skippin, avoidin the cracks. The pavin stones were big and she'd a special rhythm which nearly always worked: one-two-three-jump . . . and she was ower. Amy's breath rose in white clouds intae the bitter night.

'Mammy, could your nose freeze and turn intae an icicle?'

'Don't think so, pet.'

'How no?'

'It's no cauld enough.'

'But if it did get cauld enough, could it break aff?'

'Naw. Are you cauld?'

'Just ma nose.'

She covered it wi her white mitt.

A vision of warmth, a fire, a mug of hot tea rose afore Sandra's eyes.

'We could come back and see the lights another night.'

'Naw, Mammy, naw, we cannae go hame noo, we're nearly there, you promised . . .'

'All right, we'll go. Ah just thought you were too cauld.'

Amy had been gaun on aboot the lights for weeks; at least this would get it ower and done wi. God, she was sick of it all, specially the extra hours in the shop. Every Christmas they opened longer and longer.

Late-night shoppers, trippin ower wan another tae buy presents that'd be returned on Boxin Day, everybody in a bad mood, trachled wi parcels. And those bloody Christmas records playin non-stop. The extra hours meant extra money, right enough, and it wouldnae be so bad if they'd only tell you in advance, but see if that old bag of a supervisor sidled up tae her once more wi her 'Could you just do an extra couple of hours tonight, Sandra?' Wanny these days she'd hit her ower the heid wi a gift-wrapped basket of Fruits of Nature toiletries.

No the night, though.

'Awful sorry, Linda. Ah'm takin Amy tae see the lights in George Square. Ma neighbour's gaun late-night shoppin so she'll bring her in tae meet me.'

'Amy'll love that.'

Sandra was foldin a shelf of red sweaters when Amy came intae the shop, wearin her new coat. She adored that coat, specially the hood, which had a white fur-fabric ruff round the edge. When she'd first got it she walked aboot the hoose in it wi the hood up and Sandra could hardly persuade her tae take it off at bedtime. It had been dear, too much really, but Sandra always wanted Amy tae have nice things, she looked so good in them. She was a beautiful child, everybdy said so; even the old bag.

'What a pretty wee girl you are. Oh, she's got gorgeous curls, Sandra.'

She pressed a coin intae Amy's haund.

'That'll buy you some sweeties, pet.'

'What do you say, Amy?'

'Thank you very much.'

Amy placed the coin carefully inside her mitt.

They turned the corner and the cauld evaporated. The square shimmerin wi light, brightness sharp against the gloomy street. Trees frosted wi light. Lights shaped intae circles and flowers, like the plastic jewellery sets wee lassies love. Lights switchin on and off in a mad rhythm ae their ain, tryin tae look like bells ringin and snow fallin. Reindeer and Santas, holly, ivy, robins, all bleezin wi light. Amy gazed at them, eyes shinin.

'Haud my haund tight tae we get across this road. There's lots of motors here.' Sandra pulled Amy close in tae her. 'They're lovely, aren't they?'

'Uh huh.' Amy nodded. 'Can we walk right round the square?'

A tape of Christmas carols was playin on the sound system, fillin the air like a cracklin heavenly choir. Sandra and Amy joined the other faimlies wanderin round.

'Look at they reindeer, Mark!'

'There's a star, Daddy!'

'Check the size a that tree!'

Amy stopped in front of the big Christmas tree in the centre of the square.

'Can we sit doon tae look at it, Mammy?'

'Naw, just keep walkin, pet. It's too cauld.'

Anyway, nearly every bench was occupied. Newspapers neatly smoothed oot like bedclothes. Some folk were huddled under auld coats, tryin tae sleep their way intae oblivion while others sat upright, haufempty cans in their haunds, starin at the passers-by. Sandra minded when she was wee and her mammy'd brought her tae see the lights. There were folk on the benches then, down-and outs, faces shrunk wi drink and neglect, an auld cap lyin hauf-heartedly by their sides. But now the people who slept in the square werenae just auld drunks and it was hard tae pick them oot fae everyone else. That couple ower there wi their bags roond them, were they just havin a rest fae their Christmas shoppin, watchin the lights? But who in their right minds would be sittin on a bench in George Square on this freezin cauld night if they'd a hame tae go tae?

Amy tugged at her airm. 'Ah know that song.'

'Whit song?'

'That one.' Amy pointed upwards. 'Silent Night, Holy Night.'

'Do you?'

'We learned it at school. Mrs Anderson was tellin us aboot the baby Jesus and how there was nae room at the inn so he was born in a stable.'

'Oh.'

'It's no ma favourite, but.'

'What's no your favourite?'

'Silent Night. Guess what ma favourite is?'

'Don't know.'

'Guess, Mammy, you have tae guess.'

Sandra couldnae be bothered guessin but she knew there'd be nae peace tae she'd made some attempt and anyway, Amy'd get bored wi the 'Guess what?' game quick enough.

'Little Donkey?'

'Naw.'

'O Little Town of Bethlehem?'

'Naw. Gie in?'

'OK.'

'Away in a Manger. Ah've won!' Amy jumped up and doon. 'Mammy, what's a manger?'

'It's a thing animals eat oot of.'

'Like the cat's bowl? But that wouldnae be big enough for a baby tae sleep in.'

'Naw, it's a kind of wooden thing . . . look, there's the statues of the baby Jesus and Mary and Joseph ower there. We'll go and look at them and you can see the manger. And then,' Sandra spoke firmly so Amy wouldnae start whingein. 'We're gaun hame.'

This year the nativity scene was bigger than life-sized. The figures were bronze statues, staunin on a carpet of straw and surrounded by what looked like a hoose made of glass. It was placed tae wan side of the square, inside a fence. Sandra thought it was quite dull lookin. Weans liked bright colours and these huge people were kind of scary. She minded the wee plastic figures of Mary and Joseph she used tae set carefully in place every Christmas, leavin the baby Jesus tae last. They'd fitted intae the palm of her haund. She'd need tae get a crib for Amy. Sandra wisnae very religious, no religious at all, really, but still, it was nice for wee ones tae have a crib.

'Is that the manger, Mammy?' Amy pointed.

'That's right. D'you know who all the people are?'

Amy sucked at her mitt and looked carefully at the figures. 'That's Mary and that's Joseph – and that's the baby Jesus. And that's a shepherd wi his sheep. But who's that, Mammy?'

'They're the three wise kings. Look – they've got presents for the baby Jesus.'

'But who's *that*, Mammy? Behind the cow.'

Huddled in the straw, hidden in a corner behind the figure of a large beast, lay a man. He was slightly built, dressed in auld jeans and a thin jaicket. One of his feet stuck oot round the end of the statue and on it was a worn trainin shoe, the cheapest kind they sold in the store. Sandra moved round tae get a better look at him. He was quite young, wi a pointed face and longish dark hair. A stubbly growth covered his chin. He seemed sound asleep.

'Is he an angel, Mammy?'

Sandra didnae answer. She was lookin at the glass structure wonderin how on earth he'd got in. One of the panels at the back looked a bit loose, but you'd think they'd have an alarm on it. Lucky for him they never – at least he'd be warm in there. She was that intent on the glass panels that she'd nearly forgotten he wisnae a statue. Suddenly he opened his eyes. They were grey.

Amy grabbed her mother's arm and started jumpin up and down. 'Mammy, look, he's alive! Look Mammy. He's an angel!'

'Naw, he's no an angel. He's a man.'

'But, Mammy, what's he daein in there wi the baby Jesus?'

'Ah don't know. Mibbe he's naewhere tae stay.'

'How no, Mammy?'

'Ah don't know, Amy. Some folk don't have anywhere tae stay.'

Sandra didnae want her tae know, she was too young. She wished she could of thought of a story — he's a security guard havin a sleep, he's a councillor checkin how they've spent the ratepayers' money, he's an art student examinin the statues.

Amy stared at the man, her heid tae one side. 'He could come and stay wi us.'

'Naw, he cannae.'

'How no?'

'Because we havenae got room.'

'We have so, Mammy, we've got a spare room.'

'Aye but that's where your granny sleeps when she comes tae stay. She's comin for Christmas soon.'

'Ah can sleep wi Granny. Ah like sleepin wi ma granny. She's fat.'

'Don't tell her that.'

'How no? She's like a big hot-water bottle.'

Sandra laughed. 'C'mon.'

She took Amy's haund but Amy stayed where she was.

'If ah slept wi ma granny the man could have ma bed.'

'Naw, he couldnae. You cannae just take anybdy intae your hoose. We don't know him.'

'If he came tae stay wi us we would know him.'

'Once and for all, he's no comin hame wi us. And if you don't stop gaun on aboot it Santa'll no come this year either.' She took Amy by the haund and led her away oot the square.

At the bus stop they stood in silence, watchin the traffic crawl along the street, frost sparklin in the headlights, buses and cars filled wi parcels and exhausted shoppers. Folk scanned the number on each bus, afraid they'd miss theirs in the dark. A girl made her way alang the bus queue, a pile of papers in her airms. Sandra felt a flake of snow cauld on her cheek. She rummled in her purse, pulled oot three pound coins.

'Here.'

'Thanks.'

'Here, Amy, this is our bus.'

The bus was full and Amy sat on Sandra's knee, while a wumman squeezed intae the seat next tae them, her lap overflowin wi parcels.

'This is murder, so it is. Ah'll be glad when it's all over. Gets worse every year.'

'Aye,' said Sandra. She looked oot the windae as the bus crossed the bridge. Somehow she always felt at hame once they were ower the river though they'd still a fair bit tae go. The windae was filthy and smeared wi light fae the streetlamps. The shudderin of the bus on the potholes, the heat of the wifie next tae her, the weight of Amy as she started tae doze against Sandra's shoulder. Sandra looked doon at her sleepin bairn, eyelashes delicate on the flushed skin, then oot again through the windae, intae the dark night.

# THE DOLL'S HOUSE

Her daddy made the doll's house. She remembered sitting on a high stool next tae him at the green Formica table, watching. She couldnae remember him actually building it, sawing the bits of wood and fitting them intae place, she just remembered his concentration; head bent, the meticulous way he did the details, the fireplace in the living room, the plastic covering on the floors. And most of all, the blood gushing fae her cut thumb when she'd touched some sharp bit of metal she shouldnae of touched.

She still had the scar, L-shaped wi a thick raised piece of flesh just above it. He'd washed it oot wi some stingy stuff though she was too shocked by the blood tae notice the pain, then he'd sat her on his knee and pressed hard on the wound, a clean white hanky folded up under his fingers. He'd sat for ages, pressing on it while the red stain got bigger and bigger and he had tae take it off and replace it wi a fresh wan. Her mammy standing by holding oot a clean hanky saying she's gonnae need stitches it's that deep, you'll never stop that. But he did. And he never said you shouldnae of been so careless like he would usually.

The doll's house had been in her mammy's loft all these years. But seeing it again was as if it was yesterday, though stour was thick in the corners and the light no longer worked. A light, wi a switch on the roof that you could turn on and off. The final touch. Maybe she could wire it up again – it might just be a fuse or that. Or maybe she shouldnae try. It could be too dangerous for him, he was too young. And the wires were old. Nowadays everybody was that obsessed about their weans' safety. Socket covers and safety gates everywhere.

Funny how she never really worried aboot him though. No really. No deep down. Even when she was away fae him she felt he was wi her, as if she still cairried him inside. She was the only mother she knew who didnae have a mobile so she could be contacted at any moment. Somehow she felt nothing bad could ever happen tae him. No that she'd always been that way. When he was really wee, weeks and months auld, it had hurt her tae be away fae him even for an hour, a pain rising inside. She'd went oot noo and again, because you had tae, but she never felt right, even though at times she thought she'd go mad if she didnae get away.

She lifted off the roof. He'd designed the house hissel and it only had one storey, no like maist doll's houses where the front came off. You could change the rooms about too; only wan of the partition walls was fixed. The rest of them were made tae slot intae grooves so you could decide if you wanted wan bedroom or two, or you could take away the wall between the living room and kitchen, make it open-plan. Open-plan was dead modern then.

The wallpaper must of been modern then too. Ferny-greyish-greeny shades. Leftover bits fae their ain house, though she didnae recognise any of the patterns. She was gonnae strip the walls and paint them instead. She'd bought they wee matchpots out of Woolies. She wished she didnae have tae take oot her daddy's work though – the trouble he must of went tae, putting wee borders round the doors. She dipped the sponge intae the basin of warm water, ready tae start soakin the walls, then stopped. She'd wait till the morn, till the wee fella could watch.

His eyes were like saucers. Even if it ended in tears, even if he knocked

ower the water or got hissel covered in paint and she'd tae put the whole
lot away and listen tae his girnin, it would of been worth it just tae see
that look on his wee face.

She'd spread newspapers on the floor, tellt him no tae touch, just
watch. She was surprised when he did, sitting just off the edge of the
paper.

'My no touch,' he said, shaking his head.

'You no touch. Good boy.'

The wallpaper came dead easy, peelin aff in a wanner. She put it in a
poly bag. The stuff on the floor tae, sticky-back plastic they called it on
*Blue Peter* cos they werenae allowed tae say Fablon – that'd be adver-
tising. None of your product placement then. She wondered where her
daddy'd got it. He wouldnae of bought it special. Nothing was bought
special for a thing like this – everything was left ower. All they wee jars
wi leftower lard in them, scraped aff the pan and allowed tae solidify.
Creamy like wax, sometimes wi bits of crusted food left in them. Sitting
up on the counter tae be re-used. She could never bear tae look at them.
She threw everything oot noo, nothing got kept. Use it or lose it. Every
couple of month a clear oot, bin bags tae the charity shop. Her mammy
was shocked by it. But that skirt's hardly worn. Ah've bought a new
wan. Wan in wan oot. But she didnae remember they patterns on
anything in the hoose. Red and black on white. Fifties, almost retro
nowadays. She'd of quite liked tae keep it but it came off as soon as she'd
soaked the paper.

He was holding the paints now, gathering them up in his arms.

'My helpen.'

'That's it. You're a great help tae yer mammy.'

He was that quiet, just watching. Once she started painting no doubt
it'd be different. Once she started painting he'd put his fingers in everything, messing up. She wished she could let him just make a mess,

guddle about clarted wi paint and mud and all the other stuff. It'd be her fault if he turned oot a screwed-up neurotic. She didnae really mind mess anyway; mess could be cleaned, floors hoovered, clothes washed. It was disorder that really got her. At her work she had different sections for her paper clips, tacks, pencils. She hated places where things gathered, hated thae wee bowls where things got put if they didnae belong anywhere, like pins you'd picked up fae the floor, loose change, rubber bands the postie left lying in the close, things that were in transit or didnae belong anywhere. She liked things tae belong somewhere, tae have a place.

At night, when he went tae his bed, she spent ages putting away his toys. She couldnae just lift them up and heap them intae a box like other folk did. She had tae find the separate bits of each toy: all the jigsaw puzzle had tae go in wan box, the wee piggies' houses and the piggies in another. Worst of all was thon circus wi all the keys where you had tae turn a different key for every door. She used tae hide that sometimes so he wouldnae take it out too near bedtime. She hated when her mammy watched him, she just let him play wi everything, pulling wan thing oot and then another, guddling everything up on the floor. You could never find anything efter that. She always put wan toy back when he started playing wi another, finding all the pieces. Jesus, she was aff her heid.

'The living room's going tae be lilac. Look.'

She peeled the sealing strip fae the wee tub, lifted off the top. The paint had separated, swirls of deep purple and white; she had tae stir it round wi a wooden stick. And it was darker than she'd thought. She dipped the brush, started tae cover the living room. Maybe it'd dry lighter. You could never tell how a colour would look till you put it on; the pictures on the side were nae use. That was how she bought so many of these matchpots, trying tae get it right. She saw colours in her heid, saw them that vivid she spent ages trying tae find the right match. Wan time she'd spent a year trying tae find a shade of yellow for the hall; dark yellow it had tae be, no lemon, no orange, she'd know it when she seen it. She kept buying matchpots and trying them out on the wall behind the cupboard but they were never right so she'd try sumpn else. Eventually she gave up and painted the it coral pink instead. Even when she'd finished a room she'd aye be thinkin on another way a daein it. She'd buy a wee paint tub, lift a picture or a bit of furniture and try it oot underneath. Jesus, she was definitely aff her heid.

'Orange,' he said. 'My hold orange.'

'Aye, you hold the orange.'

She thought of orange for the hall.

'Do you want the hall tae be orange?'

'Uh huh. My room orange.'

She'd painted his bedroom orange. She wasnae sure if it worked in the daytime, but at night when she was putting him tae bed, it was that warm and womb-like in the glow of the night-light she didnae want tae leave. He was still in his cot but there was a bed in the room for when he was bigger. She'd got it fae her auntie's house when she'd flitted; a good bed, nearly new, and she just wanted tae lie down on it and fall asleep in the orange glow. She wished he still slept beside her. Some nights she'd thought of liftin him tae sleep in her bed like he did when he was a wee baby, but he slept that well in his cot she was feart tae disturb him. She missed him though, the sound of his breathing close by, his wee warm body next tae hers.

The other mothers that picked up their weans fae the nursery were all either expectin or had their next baby now, but there'd be nae second chance for her. She'd never feel that again, that precious clingin baby stage. She minded wan night when he couldnae sleep and she'd sat up on the couch wi him all night; propped up wi cushions and him lyin across her chest, dozin and sookin all night long.

And look at him now; sitting there haudin the paint in his airms.

The lilac was finished. She wiped the brush on the newspaper then folded it inside a piece of tinfoil. She wouldnae bother tae wash it the now; that wall'd be ready for another coat in a couple of hours.

Her daddy would of washed the brush out as soon as he'd finished wi it. All his brushes were perfect, lasted for years. Still they must of been a lot dearer then. Now you could buy a pack of ten for £2.99 and chuck them in the bin after the decoratin was finished. But she was just as meticulous as he'd been about the actual painting. A perfect straight line between the living room and the kitchen. The wee fella was still watching, fascinated. It was amazing he hadnae even tried tae put his fingers on the paint.

'That's the living room finished, son. Can you give me the orange and I'll dae the hall?'

'My room orange.'

'That's right, your room's orange.'

He handed her the tub of orange paint and she gave him the lilac one back.

'And the hall in the wee house is going tae be orange too.'

'My room orange.'

'Uh huh.'

'Uh huh.' He started tae put the tubs of paint on top of each other.

'Yer mammy's daddy made this house for me. Your grandfather. You've never met him . . . oh, never mind.'

It was too complicated tae explain. How tae make him understand a grandfather he'd never seen and would never see. Who would never see him.

Funny though, it never really seemed tae her he was dead. It was 20 year ago, yet if he'd walked in that door now she wouldnae of been surprised. Only last year she'd found hersel standin in a shop two days afore Christmas, wondering what tae get him. Yet in the day tae day she hardly thought of him.

'The bears can live in the house when it's finished.'

His bear family were about two inches high, just the right size for the doll's house. He was always playing with them: Daddy Bear in a blue jacket and bow tie, Mammy Bear in a blue frock and a white pinny, and Baby Bear, whom he called Teddy Boy, in his red jumper. Goldilocks completed the set but she frequently disappeared and was found days later in the back of his lorry or down the side of the settee. A free spirit. Maybe it was the blonde hair.

He had lined up the bears at the edge of the wooden board which formed the base of the house. He lifted Mammy Bear, edging her towards the door. She couldnae expect him tae just sit and watch for much longer. Anyway, the orange was finished and she couldnae tackle another colour till it dried.

'Look, son, let's put the wee house away till the paint dries. We'll need tae get the tea ready.'

She dreamed of her daddy that night, for the first time in years. She was in the kitchen of their old house, her mammy's house now, at the top of a ladder, painting the ceiling lilac. He came in the back door, his raincoat dripping with water. He took it off, shook it out, hung it on the back of the door. He crossed the kitchen till he got tae the ladder, then looked up, squinted.

'You've misssed a bit,' he said.

She could even smell paint when she woke up. She loved the smell of paint, its freshness, clean slicing through a room. She thought that different colours smelled different, but that was just daft.

The sky was grey, pressing down on her. The flat was so dark on days like this – she hated being on the ground floor, but it was so much easier when he was born; wheeling a pram straight in off the road, no having tae carry bags of messages and a baby up four flight of stairs. But she missed the airy top flat – being able tae look out and see the weather fleeing across the skies.

He sat at his wee red table, eating his toast. She loved the way he ate it, shoving it intae his mouth almost whole, devouring it.

'Go tae park mamma?' he said wi his mouth full.

'Let's go on the train the day, son, let's go intae town. It's no very nice outside.'

'Dark,' he nodded.

He loved going on the train, knelt up on the seat and gave a running commentary about everything he could see.

'Look mamma look – a digger . . . look mamma look – a taxi . . . look mamma look – a castle.'

'A castle?' She looked up fae her paper and oot the windae. Across the river was a highrise block of flats.

When she was wee they'd called them skyscrapers. They had them in New York and if you went up tae the top of them you could touch the sky. When she was eight she'd won a prize at school for writing a poem about going on a magic carpet tae visit them. She could still remember when the council had started tae build the first block of highrise flats in the town. She'd stood, haudin her daddy's hand, watching the cranes working on them, higher and higher. Can we go and stay there when they get built? No, hen. How no, daddy? We're fine where we are.

'A castle, mamma. Like Punzel.'

'Rapunzel' was one of his favourite stories. They read it nearly every night. Rapunzel, Rapunzel, let down your golden hair. She loved the surreal illustrations, they were that different fae the usual ones in kiddies' books. Rapunzel lived in a squinty tower wi bright pink walls and a checky black and white floor. The prince was a toty wee guy that Punzel could of lifted wi wan haund; she was tall and skinny as a beanpole wi yellow plaits that hung like ropes out of the tower windae. Punzel and the baby, the wee fella called them.

He was still staring out the windae.

'Who painted the sky, mamma?'

'God.'

She didnae think she really believed in God but she minded how comforting it was when she was wee, knowing He was up there in the sky, watching over her.

'He gets fed up wi it though, changes the colours every day.' She pointed across the city. 'See that patch there – it's lighter than the rest of the grey – he must be painting that the now . . .'

'Look, look, what's that, mamma?'

Far in the distance, a ball of fire seemed tae fall fae the sky.

When they got home she turned on the news, wanting tae find oot what it was – a bit off a plane, some kind of explosion maybe – but there was nothing. She wondered if she'd imagined it. It was huge, must of done some damage falling out of the sky, surely they'd put it on the news. And it must of been real. As soon as they'd got in, he'd taken his colouring pencils oot and started tae draw it on a bit of paper, making circles wi orange and red and yellow.

The house was nearly finished now; she'd put two coats of paint on every surface and varnished the floors. She'd tried tae get Fablon tae cover them but couldnae find the right shade, so she'd just painted them instead. It was touching up that was needed now, the odd trace of paint in the wrong place, a line here and there that could be straighter, and it was easier tae dae the footery bits when he was in his bed.

She was dead chuffed with it now. Fae the outside it didnae look any different, just smarter; she'd kept the same colours – white walls and a red roof. But when you opened it up, it was loupin with colour: lilac living room, lime-green kitchen, orange hall, blue bathroom, coral-pink bedrooms. She took oot the box of furniture she'd bought. She didnae know what had happened tae the auld furniture she'd had and, anyway, she wanted him tae have new stuff. These pieces were all made of wood, modern and brightly coloured. There was even a wooden pot of tulips tae go in the middle of the coffee table. She placed them carefully in each room. The colour scheme in the living room was really wild; orange and yellow chairs against the lilac walls – the folk on these decorating shows on the TV would love it. She'd never watched any of them herself, hardly watched the TV at all, but her mammy loved them. Every week when she came round tae watch him she'd go on about how awful the previous night's one was – wait tae her mammy saw the dolls' house. But her daddy would of liked it, she was sure. Did like it. Nae doubt he was watching, somewhere.

The bears were watching her, lined up in a row on the top of the bookcase. She picked them up and stood them outside the wee house. One by one she walked them inside, Mammy Bear first, then Baby Bear, then Daddy Bear. She sat them in the chairs in the living room, then moved them around; Teddy Boy in the bathroom having a bath, Daddy Bear making a cup of tea, Mammy Bear going intae the hall. Time for bed, bears. But there were only two beds in the house, one in each bedroom. They were both the same size. She sat for a minute, holding the bears in her left hand. Then she placed Mammy Bear in the bed in the front bedroom and Teddy Boy in the bed in the back bedroom. Night, said Daddy Bear, and walked out through the front door. She put the roof on the house, lifted Daddy Bear back on tae the top of the bookcase.

His truck was lying in front of the fire, over on one side. She turned it round the right way, fished deep into the back behind the driver's seat. She was there. She poked her fingers in, fiddling till Goldilocks fell out. She placed her on the bookcase next tae Daddy Bear. Night night, bears. She switched off the light and left the room.

# BRAMBLING

Light sliced through the trees, picking out spiders' webs between the branches. The wind had felt fresh and strong before they'd entered the woods but now only a mild breeze ruffled the leaves. As usual, they had on too many clothes; she'd dressed him in his bright green fleece and put on her pink one, thinking they would need protection against the wind, forgetting how enclosed it was here.

The road that led from the gates was scarred with scummy puddles. He splattered their cloudy rainbows with his feet. You could almost touch the quiet; yards away from a main road, ten minutes' drive from their house in the heart of the city, but once you were inside it was as if you were right in the countryside. She'd never been here with him on her own before; occasionally, the three of them came on Sunday afternoons when it was busier; families feeding the squirrels, walking dogs.

Fridays were a gift. She worked four days a week so on her day off they'd always do something special; jump in the car and go down the coast, get on a bus and travel across the city, go to a café for lunch. He was the age where everything was fun so she'd follow her instincts, avoid chores or shopping, just head. And this morning when she saw the blue sky splashed with clouds, she knew it would be perfect for brambling.

'Big trees.'

He held her hand at first, staring upwards. They came to a gate that opened on to an expanse of grass. A woman was walking her dog just on the other side.

'Look look mamma, a doggy.'

'So there is. Let's go and say hello.'

'Hello, doggy.'

The woman smiled as he stared at the dog, who snuffled past showing no interest in him. They turned off to the left along a track next to the fence.

'We'll find lots here.'

She scanned the tangled undergrowth. Big leaves with black spots on them. Always gave her the creeps.

'Look, there they are – brambles.'

'Bambles.'

She took two plastic tubs from her bag.

'D'you want to carry one?'

A big smile.

'Sam got a tub.'

'You've got a tub. Look, this is what you do.'

She crouched down close to the fence where a branch held out its clump of berries.

'See the red ones – they're not ready yet so you don't pick them.'

'No.'

'It's the black ones we want. You pull them and if they're ready they'll just come.'

She tugged one that came away easily. Funny how you couldn't tell from looking which ones were ready. Sometimes they seemed quite ripe but weren't, while others yielded at the first touch.

He put out his finger and stroked one of the berries. She knew he was too wee to understand but she always liked to explain things to him. Anyway it didn't matter – she could dump the ones that weren't good enough. She started to pick, searching the guddle of leaves and branches, turning them over – the best ones were often sheltering on the underside. He stood close by, tentatively pulling at berries till one came off in his hand.

'Look, mamma, look, Sam got a bamble.'

He held it up, his face as excited as if he'd been given a present.

'Well done. Put it in your bowl. See if you can get some more. Look – down there. You can reach them.'

She edged along, reaching right into the bushes, stretching for those further away. She hated to see the ones that had already died, shrivelled up unpicked. It was a shame more folk didn't come brambling; there were plenty here.

'Look, mamma, look.'

He held up a bright red berry, obviously unripe.

'Just throw it away, pet. It's not ready.'

He chucked it into the undergrowth using all his strength, then turned to face her. Caught in a patch of sunlight, he held out his bowl with one bramble in it, a big smile on his face. She wished she'd brought the camera.

'Let's go on a bit further. We'll get some more.'

He ran towards her and she took his hand. They turned a bend in the road and found their way blocked.

'What's that, mamma?'

'It's a car, son.'

A cold feeling in the marbled light. The burnt-out shell of a car skewed across the path. She'd never seen one close up, only glimpsed them in passing at the side of the road. How on earth had it got here? As she looked, she realised it was not one, but two cars compressed. They must come joyriding here at night. A sudden vision of the forest at night; pitch black pinpricked by headlights, motors screaming along the path then crash — one ramming the other. Close up she saw that the insides were completely burnt out, like the bones of an animal picked clean by vultures. They must smash them up then set them on fire deliberately, for fun. Young boys standing round with cans in their hands watching cars spark and roar; flames leaping into the dark night, heat searing their faces.

She wondered if they should try another route. They couldn't get past the cars unless they climbed up the bank opposite and it looked too steep for him. But if they turned back they'd have to go a long way round to find more brambles and he'd get tired.

'Let's go round this way and see what it's like.'

She pushed him up the brae in front of her, finding wee footholds, him laughing and giggling. Then they walked a few yards round the the cars and scrambled back down the slope away from them without looking back. Further on they reached a rough set of steps which led down to an open area of grass.

'Down steps.'

'Yes, we'll go down the steps. This is lovely here — look at the trees.'

She wished she knew more about trees, could tell him the different kinds, but she was hopeless. All the ones in the forest they'd passed had been green but these were turning spicy colours; cinnamon, saffron, ginger. Leaves freckled the grass. A man walked a labrador dog. An old couple wandered arm in arm towards the pitches. She continued picking, filling another tub, while he ran about on the grass, swishing his wellies through the damp leaves.

'Don't go too far. We'll be going soon.'

'Look, mamma, Sam's hands red.'

His hands were stained with mauve, the lines in his palm etched deep purple. Headline, heartline, lifeline. She could never remember which was which. Her own hands were perforated by bramble thorns and streaked with pink.

'It's OK, it's just the brambles. It'll wash off.'

She put the plastic lid on the tub and placed it in the bag.

'That should be enough. You can help me make crumble tonight'.

'Sam make cumble.'

'We'll need to go and get some flour, though. We'll stop at the shops on the way home.'

'Daddy get cumble.'

'Daddy loves crumble.'

She took his hand. After a few steps he turned to her and put his arms round her legs.

'Carry up, mamma.'

'You tired?'

He was a ton weight. The quickest way out was to go along the path near the river for a few yards, then cut off towards the main gates, but all these tracks looked the same, framed by monumental trees. Last time they'd ended up wandering round in circles before finding the right one. She couldn't afford to do that today, not with him so tired.

She set him down on the ground.

'Let's play that we're the babes in the woods. We'll put a trail of bread on the ground so if we get lost we'll know which way we've come.'

She took out the bag of bread she'd brought to feed the birds and started to pick bits from it. She gave him a slice and he pulled off a big lump.

'No, son, just wee bits – we don't want to use up all the bread right away.'

They continued along the path, dropping the bread behind them. It was darker now, the only light high up in the treetops. They should be heading upwards now, towards the main road, but they seemed to be going down. It was like a maze in here.

'I think we need to go back a bit, pet, try another path. Let's see if we can get back to that place where the big log was. If we go right there I'm sure that'll take us out of the woods.'

She wasn't sure at all but there were only so many ways it could be.

'Carry up.'

She lifted him, going slowly, watching for the scraps of bread at the side of the path till they reached a clearing, a crossroads. She remembered this one. Three tracks led out of it.

'I think we came this way.'

The trail of bread had disappeared completely. But she knew this wasn't where they'd started off.

'Where's the bread? It should be here.'

'Birdies got it.'

'I don't think so, pet.'

She'd never seen a bird in these woods. Squirrels, never birds. She'd never thought of it before. Squirrels don't eat bread.

'Let's try this one.'

More trees, The track was muddier though, her feet sinking slightly at each step. Maybe that meant they were near the river. If they could follow it they'd definitely find their way out even if it took them longer.

'Could you walk for bit, pet?'

'Carry up.'

He was so heavy. She'd never manage to carry him all the way. But there was a patch of light here, an opening. Leaves brittle under her feet.

'Hey, Sam, this is the place we were before. With the lovely trees.'

'Brown trees.'

'Gold.'

They could cross over and go up the steps, return the way they'd come; even though it'd take a while, at least she knew where they were, they'd have a definite route to follow. But they'd have to go past the cars again.

Light sliced through the trees, picking out spiders' webs between the branches. The wind had felt fresh and strong before they entered the woods but now only a mild breeze ruffled the leaves. They lay face down, he curled close into her side, their hands scored purple-red. As usual they had on too many clothes; she had dressed him in his bright green fleece and put on her pink one, thinking they would need protection against the wind, forgetting how enclosed it was here.

# THE WORKSHOP

Oose covered the wall bars and nestled into the skirting board. A fusty smell hung in the air. Each week the boiler creaked into life for a few hours and, though the air never quite lost its chill edge, the flaking radiators would grow too hot to touch.

A guy wearing a grubby lab coat let her in, then paused in the doorway.

'What time d'you finish?'

'I think about four. The kids and their teacher are due to arrive at two. I wanted to be here a bit early, check the place out before they arrived.'

His eyes scanned the room.

'You a drama teacher, then?'

'I'm just running some workshops for a school drama club. I'm a student at the drama school. Mature student.'

He crossed the room and bent down to one of the radiators, felt it with the palm of his hand. 'Getting there.'

His face was round and crumpled, like a cartoon baby.

'We used to get a lot of schools doing drama here.'

'Not now?'

'This place is on its last legs. The council want to knock it down but the building's listed so they have to let it rot away a bit first.'

He leaned his back against the radiator.

'I'm just clearing stuff out. Old TVs and tape recorders. I'm an AV technician for the local schools.'

He crossed the room and stood beside her, fumbling in his trouser pocket. 'Look, if you don't mind, I've a few things to do this afternoon and I think I'll go off a bit early.' He held out a round metal keyring with two keys attached.

'Sure. How do I get these back to you?'

'You hold on to that set till you finish your workshops. How many you doing?'

'Six — it's six weeks altogether.'

'Fine. Just stick the keys through the letterbox after the last one.'

'OK.'

'Means you can come and go as you please. Saves me being here every Friday afternoon.'

'Thanks.'

'Good luck with the workshops.'

Workshops. Why *workshops*? It was a stupid name. She'd never thought of it before, why think of it here, lying in the near silence, slivers of sound, slats of blinds tapping the frame in the breeze from the window. Why now, when he said, 'What are you thinking?' — why that instead of something profound and tender?

'Workshops.'

He lay on his side, his arm across her, fingers stroking the bruise above her hip bone. It was purple and yellow now, less angry than it had been last week. She couldn't even remember how she'd got it; she bruised so easily that a bump from a door handle or a table edge could leave her black and blue for weeks.

'What about them?'

'Why they're called that. I mean, it's a daft name.'

'Yeah, daft.'

She tried to look at her watch without moving but he caught her glance.

'Sorry, I have to pick up Robbie at half past today.'

'I know. It's OK.'

She traced a finger round his left eyebrow, looked into his eyes.

He smiled. 'Really OK.'


There was a thunderstorm that night. Standing at the window, watching the sky spark and crash, she felt relief. It must have been the build-up of pressure before the storm that had caused her to feel so strange earlier on; she was sensitive to changes in atmosphere, hated the heavy low cloud which passed for summer in the city. Every other time she'd been so abandoned, lost in the moment, but today she'd felt a presence in the room, as though her mind was outside her body watching them on the floor. Making love, if you could call it that. But what else would you call it?

She wrapped her dressing gown tighter round her, placed her middle finger on her mouth, pressing it against her lower lip. Next week would be the last workshop.


It was when they froze and locked eyes that she'd known they'd do it. In the middle of the improvisation when everyone was freaking out, screaming and jumping; someone, one of the kids shouted, 'Stop!' Rooted to the spot, she, finding herself six inches away from him, looked up into his eyes and knew.

Afterwards, when they were dropping off the kids, Jack, one of the last group, banged on the window of the minibus and waved. He'd turned to look at her with a smile of such openness, partly for the boy and partly for her, that it seemed as though they had planned for him to drive back to the centre and for her to unlock the door, then lock it again behind them, and for them to lie down on the dusty floor together.

The warmth of his body shocked her; he had looked so cool in the pale blue denim shirt. That heat was what she remembered, and the silence. They must have made a noise but she wasn't aware of it. The world had concentrated into one place, the one place where he stayed, making slight movements, keeping her just at the edge. Light filtered through her half-closed eyes. She let him do as he wished, as she wished, but how did he know? And the edge, round the edge, like a finger rimming a glass till it tingles, till it builds, till it rings out, rings a clear note – oh. Then a deeper note joining, and she felt his weight and his forehead damp against hers.

Suddenly her body was heaving, shuddering with laughter; he took his weight off her and she rolled onto her side, helpless.

'I'm sorry . . . I'm not laughing at you . . . I . . .'

'That wasn't quite the effect I had in mind.'

She smiled, touched his mouth with her finger. 'Couldn't help it . . . it was just so fucking good.'

For those few hours in the week she'd had nothing to think about, nothing to do.

'It's like I'm just my body, nothing else, totally in my body.'

'I thought it was me who was in your body.'

'Typical male. Take all the credit.'

'OK, we were both in your body – have it your own way.'

'That reminds me of that awful lorry-driver joke.'

'Go on.'

'Ach, I can't remember it all but the punchline is he meets someone else inside looking for his motor bike.'

'If that's the punchline, I don't think I want to hear the joke. Anyway, let's get back to your body.'

'Only if I can get back to yours.'

'It's a deal.'

So they'd never got round to talking about it. And there was no one else she could talk to, didn't want to anyway. It wouldn't make sense.

Occasionally, they did talk about their other lives. He had two kids, a bit older than Robbie, was married.

'We never bothered. Just as well really, as it turned out.'

'How long ago d'you split up?'

'Four years. Robbie doesn't really know much different. Still sees his dad a lot.'

Robbie's jigsaw puzzle lay on the table; he'd been working on it for days now. It was too difficult for him, with too many pieces, and the picture was of an old-fashioned cottage with a thatched roof and roses round the door. Hardly what you'd choose for a seven-year-old. Why on earth had her mother bought it?

She picked up a piece of sky and fitted it along the outer edge. Another slotted in below. Blue sky with fluffy white clouds. Subtle shading and tone. She could do some of the sky and leave him the easier bits. They were more fun anyway; the cottage with its shuttered windows and red door, the flower bed with poppies and lavender. There were some animals in the picture and he'd be so chuffed when he found the piece with the cat on it.

She sat down at the table, shuffled all the blue parts round on its surface and started to sort clouds.

'So, next week.'

The sun made long straight lines on the floor; dust settled, mesmerised by light.

'I don't know what to say.'

She ran her finger along the inside of his arm, paused at the crease of his elbow.

'D'you know that this is the place where you smell most of yourself? You know, like your essence.' She leaned over and put her nose there.

'Why there?'

'Don't know. Read it somewhere.'

'I'd have thought there were other places you'd smell more of yourself.'

'Where?'

'Want me to show you?'

'Only if I can show you.'

'Mine or yours?'

'What's mine is yours.'

\*

The kids were hyper.

'Haw, sir, it's the last week.'

'I know it's the last week.'

Alan had climbed the wall bars, was swinging from them by one hand and one foot.

'Haw, sir, gonnae gie's a party this week?'

'A party? I thought it was a party every week in here for you guys.'

'And for yous two.'

'Come on, Jason, we're here to work.'

'Heard it. Haw, miss, whit are we daein the day?'

'How about you do a show for us? Those improvisations you did last week. Take ten minutes to get them right and we'll watch them. OK?'

They went through their warm-up, simple stretches and breathing exercises, without any of the giggling and complaints she'd had to work against that first time, then each group took its turn.

'Well done, Andy.'

'Good work, you three.'

'That's come on a storm, girls.'

Yet all through the performances she kept glancing down to his thigh, the only part of him she could see without looking round directly. She wanted to touch him, felt the want rise till her throat was raw. It seemed such a natural thing to do, while they sat here together with their kids round them. Her leg was an inch away from his, her hand resting on her own thigh. If she just slid it down no one would notice. She looked up and saw the technician standing at the side of the room.

'I didn't expect him back. Thank god he didn't stay.'

'When did he come in?'

'I'm not sure – it was in the middle of Gina and Andy's scene when I noticed him. Spent the rest of the time trying to work out an excuse for not giving him back his keys. Can you imagine if we'd had to leave along with the kids?'

'Doesn't bear thinking about.' He slid his tongue along the nape of her neck. 'How long have you got?'

'I could stay till six, maybe six-thirty?'

He moved on top of her, touched her nose with his. 'We need to talk today.'

'I know.'

'Let's go for a drink after.'

'After.'

The squeal of feedback blasted into the room, ricocheted off the walls and ceiling, the sound amplifying then suddenly cutting dead.

'What the hell . . .' He sat up, started to pull on his jeans.

A whisper at first, then a murmur, still the words unintelligible, just sounds rising and falling, oh, oh, ah, ah, oh, then louder and clearer, oh, oh so, so fuck, fucking, oh, no, no, yes, echoing, swelling to fill each crack in the floorboards, each gap in the skirting. Then silence.

'What the fuck?'

She took his hands. 'The bastard's taped us.'

'Fucking bastard.'

'I'm scared. Let's get out of here.'

'No – I'm going to get him. I'll kill him.'

He pulled his hands away.


She'd worked her way down from the sky, down the left-hand side where the blue gave way to green trees, which merged into green grass. The green was even harder to do since there was less gradation of colour. Every now and then she left a part for Robbie: two horses looking over a fence, a few sheep in a field. Then she continued, slotting together piece after piece while the rain fell.


She wanted to go outside. It was sunny outside, the air was clean, and this placed smelled sour. She wanted to sit with him outside, on the grass under a tree, just looking at him. She never got the chance to look at all of him; either she sneaked glances when the kids were there or else they were so close she could see only strange angles of his face, isolated parts of his body. She knew him through smell and touch and taste.


Across the road from the centre was a piece of waste ground, littered with gravel and dogshit. Her legs felt weak but she didn't want to sit down so she leaned against the metal fence, watching the building. The door was at the top of a flight of stone stairs, surrounded by ornately carved lions. In a few weeks they would be smashed to rubble.

He crossed the road, carrying her blue canvas bag, ridiculously small over his shoulder.

'He's not there.'

'I'm sorry, I should've stayed.'

'Don't be daft. I found this.' He pulled a tape out of his pocket. 'The machine was plugged into one of these time-switch things. Sick bastard.'

'He must've been there, watching, listening. Oh, god . . .' She touched his arm.

'Don't. He might still be around. Let's go.'

The pub was dark and cool after the bright sunlight but the plastic of the seat felt sticky against the backs of her legs. She watched as he bought the drinks, thinking how unfamiliar he seemed. She didn't know the everyday things; the way he stood at the bar, how he held a note between his fingers.

He drank his pint in silence. There was foam on his upper lip. She wanted to kiss it off but when she leaned over the table, he put out his hand and stopped her.

'I'd better listen to that tape tonight. He may've put something else on it, maybe even a message or something.'

'It makes me feel sick to think of him listening to us, getting some twisted kicks out of . . . doesn't bear thinking about.'

'We've got to think, though. This might not be the end of it.'

'What d'you mean?'

'Well, blackmail, I suppose.'

'Blackmail – oh, for god's sake.'

'He might think it'd be worth a try. I'm a teacher – in charge of the kids, on council premises – can you imagine the headlines?'

'You don't think he'd do that?'

'You don't know what a sick bastard like that could get up to. Probably fancies you himself.'

'Don't say that.'

'I don't see why he wouldn't.'

'No – fancies.'

'Eh?'

'It's just the word, fancies . . . as if that's all it was.'

He ran his finger round the edge of his glass, wiping off the froth.

'What would you call it?'

'There isn't a word for it, that's the trouble. It doesn't fit in.'

'I thought it fitted in pretty well.'

She smiled, but without the touch that should have accompanied them, the words seemed to echo in the space between them.


She was finishing off a clump of darker trees on the edge of a field when the phone rang.

At first she didn't recognise his voice.

'It's me. Can you talk?'

'Yeah, Robbie's in his bed. Are you . . .'

'I'm phoning from a call box. Took the dog out for a walk.'

'You've got a dog?'

There was a sheepdog in the field behind the house.

'Look, I've only got 10p. I listened to the tape on my Walkman. Just more of the same.'

'Just us.'

'Yeah. Kind of turned me on, I have to say.' He laughed.

She removed the piece with the dog on it and set it to one side for Robbie.

'Pity he didn't make a video.'

'What?'

'Never mind. What d'you want to do?'

'I think we should have it out with him.'

'Can we meet first?'

'How about Tennent's – tomorrow at four?'

'OK. I . . .'

'Money's running out.'

'See you.'

What could she have said? Miss you? Desire you? Love you? What was the word? All the words brought up the wrong pictures. She didn't want to see him every day or iron his shirts or know he had a dog. She just wanted to keep the part she had.

It hadn't mattered before that there was no word. When they were together, closer than close in the warm smooth roundness, the words were irrelevant. Now, when all they had was words, the world was full of jaggy edges, sharp corners.

She knew it was a stupid thing to do, to tackle the guy by herself, but, as soon as she'd left Robbie at school that morning, she found herself heading in the direction of the centre. He walked round the corner carrying a black holdall and when he reached the steps, she crossed the road quickly.

His eyes narrowed as he turned towards her, facing the sun. 'Hi. How's it going?' Close up his skin was smooth and even in tone. 'Caught some of your workshop on Friday. Looked pretty good to me, not that I know much about acting.'

'You're doing a pretty good job just now.'

'Sorry?'

'Oh, stop it. I don't know what you thought you were doing but if there's any more copies . . .'

'I don't know what you're talking about.'

He took out a bundle of keys and placed one in the lock.

'We want them.'

'Want what?'

'You could get into trouble too. I'll tell them you gave me the keys.'

He turned the key in the lock and picked up his bag. 'Keep the keys, chuck them in the river for all I care. They're knocking this place down next week. I'm just here to get that set of lights you were using, then I'm off.'

'And the tape recorder?'

'What tape rcorder?'


Robbie had gone in a huff when he'd seen how much of the jigsaw she'd completed, but it was soon over when he realised she'd left the best bits for him. He did the horses and one of the windows of the cottage. She carried on working her way round the outside; the cornfield which formed the foreground, in shifting degrees of yellow ochre.


Sitting in the pub with him, she could feel the gap inside where the feeling used to come. She felt herself breathing round the edges of it, willing it, trying to sweep out the particles of leftover sensation and whip them into a dust storm. She wanted the feeling to flood over her, to know they were joined together as they'd been on the floor of the room.

He stared into his pint, kept pushing it backwards and forwards on the surface of the table. She watched his hands, thinner than you'd expect on a man of his build and the cuticles so white and clean; he must push them back with the corner of a towel. She was taking him in, observing every detail, knowing that they were close to the end.

He spoke without looking at her.

'It wasn't him.'

'I didn't think so. He seemed so . . . as if he really didn't know.'

'You spoke to him?'

'Went there this morning.'

'You what?'

'I had to.'

'Never mind. Doesn't matter now.'

His glass had started to slide, just slightly, in the film of liquid on the table.

'Who was it, then?'

'One of the kids. I don't know which.'

'They told you?'

'No, it was . . . when they came in today it was obvious. Nothing I could put my finger on, just the way they were sniggering and restless and . . .'

'And?'

'Then Julie said, "You really like her, sir, don't you?" and I said, "Who?" and there was a bit of muttering and I think I heard one of the boys say something about shagging – God, it's . . .'

'Are you sure? I can't believe they would . . . I mean, we used to do that at school – you know, think teachers fancied each other, but it didn't mean anything.'

'I know them. The atmosphere was so different today. I feel like shit.'

She reached for his hand, turned it palm upwards and stroked the inside of his wrist.

'So, what do we do?'

'There's nothing to do. I just have to hope they'll leave it at that. Knowing them, it'll probably all have blown over by next week. The summer holidays are coming up. Now the workshops are finished, it's less of an issue.'

She pressed her thumb against his pulse point.

'So what do we do?'

He took his hand away, pushed his hair back.

'We don't do anything.'

The cornfields gave way to trees and grass on the other side of the picture. She positioned each piece carefully, each rounded projection slotting into the equivalent hollow. Only a few more square inches to cover.

'We knew it wasn't going to last.'

'I don't think I knew anything.'

'I can't leave my kids.'

'I'm not asking you to leave them. Don't be so fucking arrogant. D'you think I don't have a life? D'you think I want you around all the time?'

'Well, what do you want?'

'I want what we had. I want for us to be . . . special to each other.'

She lifted her empty glass, replaced it a few inches away on the table.

'Surely we could go on the way we've been? You could get away for a couple of hours a week – that's all I want.'

'It wouldn't work that way. These things never do. One of us would . . . you can't keep love in a box.'

'There's a million different ways of loving someone.'

'And we only managed twelve.'

'Don't, I can't bear . . .'

'Sorry.'

The place was empty. The last few bits and pieces of furniture had gone, ready for the demolition. Taking off her sandals, she sat on the floor, tracing her foot along the shafts of light. When she heard the door open she thought at first it was the technician; kept still, as if that would make him go away. Then she smelled the familiar scent, felt his hands on her shoulders.

'How did you know?'

'Followed you here. I've been watching you all week, sitting outside your house in the car, watching your lights go on and off, imagining you moving around.'

She stood up, turned to face him.

'Why didn't you come to the door? I've missed you.'

'Me too. I know what I said, but I couldn't . . . not say goodbye properly . . .'

'Don't talk – come here.'

He must have finished it with his granny, when she was out. Blue sky, green trees, yellow cornfields, roses round the door, a cat sunning itself on the front step. Perfect, except there was a piece missing, must have fallen on the floor. She knelt down and searched the room, even moving the settee and looking behind the bookcase. Well, Robbie wouldn't care; it wasn't a very important piece anyway, just part of the sky. It would have been nice to have it complete though. She stood at the window, looking out at the night. High above the rooftops the round white moon looked in.

# MARKING TIME

Orazio was sweeping the beach.

The old-fashioned besom had started to come apart; pieces of stick and straw detaching themselves, littering the sand as he worked. It would be easier with a new brush, one of the plastic ones with soft bristles. Piero sold them in the hardware shop, but Enrico was adamant that the twigs made a better job of turning over the sand, and who was he to argue? Enrico paid him, after all.

Every evening, at around five o'clock, when the heat of the sun eased and tourists made their way back to the hotels, Orazio started at the edge of the beach nearest the sea, covering a patch about a metre across before moving along to the next one, lifting the sand, then smoothing it back into place. The sun burning his back, the ghost of a breeze tickling his face, he worked his way straight across the shoreline then moved inwards, crossing and recrossing the beach till he arrived at the umbrellas and deckchairs. By then the tourists had left and he continued sweeping while Enrico lifted the deckchairs, shaking each one out and wiping it with a cloth before carefully folding and stacking it in the hut. Once they were done, Orazio rolled up the umbrellas and secured each one with a piece of blue and red striped ribbon. Then headed across to the café to wait for Chiara.

Orazio walked through dead leaves each morning to the library, scarf shielding his throat from the sharp cold air. Brightness was rationed here. In summer the Glasgow skies were so heavy with cloud and humid air that the season was just something to be got through. But in October a flash of gold light could catch him off guard, bring it back to him.

He had not been back for twenty years. Enrico's stretch of beach was old-fashioned even twenty years ago, when the heavy wood and canvas deckchairs were being replaced by plastic-coated loungers. Enrico thought it was a phase.

'It's quality that lasts, Orazio. These guys are fly-by-night, flash — don't put in the effort. Quality and care, that's what the customers are looking for.'

Most of Enrico's customers were Italian, spending a month at the seaside in extended family groups, returning season after season. To go to any other part of the beach would be unthinkable. Yet things were changing. New hotels appeared, seemingly overnight, and the number of foreign tourists increased. These tourists didn't care about Enrico's painstakingly hand-painted sign or that he remembered their names. The neighbouring stretch of beach had been taken over by Paolo, who charged less and had a machine which sold soft drinks.

He'd heard nothing from any of them since he'd left, except Enrico. Each year, around October time, when the tourist season wound down to a halt, he received a letter addressed care of the university, the small cramped handwriting filling the page. News of his family: Assia has had another baby, a boy. Of the neighbours: Angelo has got a bigger house but people say he's drinking too much. But above all, news of the beach and Paulo: Paulo has more new loungers this year, he'd rather throw things out than spend time repairing them. Paulo has installed a computerised cash register that gives receipts. What do you need receipts for on a beach? Paulo has employed a young girl in shorts and a bikini top to take the money. How low can you get in trying to steal away custom?

*

And now Enrico was dead.

Orazio drank his coffee in one quick movement, a rush of caffeine hitting the back of his skull. He placed the envelope in his pocket, lifted his paper.

'*Ciao*, Giulio,'

'*Ciao*, Orazio, see you tomorrow.'

He stopped by the café every morning on his way to work. Usually he avoided anything that reminded him of home, but this place, where he and Giulio spoke in Italian, but casually, about the football or the weather, not touching on anything personal, made him feel at peace somehow.

Sometimes, on rare trips to the sea, he'd felt something close to peace, his lungs filling with air, eyes narrowing to take in the blue-grey shredded with silver, the vault of the sky. But it wasn't the northern waters which moved him, only a memory raised in him, of his own sea; just as the light falling on a woman's arm at a certain angle made him shut his eyes as though the brightness was too great.

He'd shut his eyes that day, when she told him, as they sat side by side on the beach, her toes snaking along the sand, making indentations.

'Hey, watch it, you're messing up my work!'

'And what're you going to do about it? How you going to punish me?'

'I'm going to tickle you.'

And he let her fall gently to the sand, leaning over her, holding her wrists, looking into her eyes.

Then she told him, and he shut his eyes, unable to bear the brightness of her face. He didn't know how to tell her, couldn't understand how she didn't see it the way he did. It was like thinking, through some trick of the light, they'd been travelling on the same road when really they were parallel ones with no convergence.

He listened. Of course, she knew it was too soon, money would be tight, she'd have to keep working while he studied. And her parents would be furious, but, they'd get over it. A baby. A baby. A gift. Her eyes shone.

He should have tried to explain to her, but how to put out that light? He didn't know. And how could she not understand? A baby. A baby. A nuisance.

Orazio found a place at the window. He placed the book in front of him on the wooden desk, scarred with graffiti. The sun was warm and Orazio shut his eyes. A murmur of movement, the crackle of turning pages, keys clanking in a pocket, each person cloistered in their own tower of paper and printing ink. This was his life.

He returned to the glossy reproductions, familiar names: Bellini, Giorgione, Titian. He'd come here to study Art History, hoping to lecture in it, but his degree wasn't good enough, there was too much competition. He'd become a librarian instead, working in the building in which he had studied, losing himself in the scent of old paper and leather-bound volumes. Now the routine jobs in the library were done by assistants and he hid behind a computer screen most of the day. Only occasionally, like today, his old skills were called upon.

'The Madonna in the Venetian Renaissance'.

Each baby playing with something which symbolised his fate: a sprig of red berries, a red flower, sometimes a bird. Each mother looking on, fearful yet resigned to her son's destiny. Most of the plates were black and white, and Orazio studied the careful delineation of folded drapery and fine features as he turned each page, occasionally marking the place with a piece of tissue paper torn from a large sheet. Then came a full-page reproduction in rich jewel colours: the Bellini Madonna he'd seen when he first arrived in Glasgow. It used to hang in the Art Galleries and he'd gone there every Sunday, not wanting to look but unable to keep away.

The background was green, a shade impossible to obtain using modern paints — probably lead-based. The Madonna was beautiful but grave; pale-skinned, un-Italian in appearance, and she watched, not her child, but the flower with which he played.

Nights spent on the beach in the lingering heat, huddled in the shadow of Enrico's hut, his arm round her, her finger tracing circles in the sand.

'I think it's a boy.'

'How can you tell? There's nothing even to see yet.'

'He'll have curly hair, like yours.'

And the days; sweeping, hearing only the swish of the brush as it passed over the dusty sand, seeing only waves skim the shore.

From the window he gazed across the city. The perspective made him lose his sense of direction and though he'd walked these streets year after year, he could no longer identify them. Tenements and tower blocks. It was an ugly city when you saw it spread out like this. Even the university buildings were fake: mock-Gothic, out of proportion, their fairy-tale towers contrasting with the highrise flats on the outskirts, the industrial debris. He could not see the river, merely sense its presence from the cranes.

Orazio took the letter out of his pocket, spread it in front of him next to the art book. It was full of legal jargon but the solicitor had attached a note.

'Enrico knew he was ill last year when he came to see me. He was most insistent that the beach was left to you, even though he had not seen you for so many years. I would be grateful if you would let me know as soon as possible your wishes regarding the property. Should you desire to sell it, Paulo Mancini, who owns the next stretch, would be prepared to make a good offer.'

Far in the distance light shimmered on rooftops. He folded the letter and replaced it in the envelope. He scrutinised the face of the Madonna but she looked down resolutely, refusing to meet his gaze. Orazio tore another strip of tissue paper from the sheet, placed it next to her and turned the page.

# A RINGIN FROST

Ah turn the gless ball in ma haun and a skimmer of white flakes birl roon the red plastic rose at its centre.

*At's nice that.*

*Aye, ah've no seen wanny them for years.*

*Whit is it?*

He's taen it oot ma haun and is turnin it roon, starin at it. He looks like a wee boy.

*It's just a Christmas decoration, for weans, really. Ah mind we had wan in the hoose when ah wis a wee lassie, a Santa it wis.*

*Much is it?*

*£6.95, it's too dear, Jimmy.*

*Ah'll buy it fur ye, hen, ah'll get it.*

And before ah kin say anythin he's aff tae the checkoot queue. That's Jimmy fur ye – aw oor lives he's been the wan gettin things, daein things, the fiery wan. Me, ah'm the wan that's held back, been mair cautious, caulder, ah suppose. Mibbe that wis the attraction between us, we were that opposite. Ah loved him right away, he wis that open, that smilin and warm. The first time he walked me hame fae the dancin and gied me a cuddle it wis lik ah big bleeze heatin me up, he's like havin yer ain eletric blanket in bed wi ye. And me, ah'm that chilly ah'd have the central heatin on in June. Ah suppose ah'm caulder in ma nature as well, cannae help it. Ah've never been wan tae let ma emotions oot, ah wis aye taught tae keep them tae masel, good and bad.

And at first it seemed that bein wi Jimmy wi his warmth and yon sparkle in his eye hud kindled me, as if ah wis a hoose wi a fire laid waitin tae be lit. We were that daft, couldnae keep wer hauns aff wan anither. Peter, oor eldest, wis a honeymoon baby and ah mind wan day when he wis aboot 16 we went a run tae Culzean Castle.

*Huvnae been here fur years.*

*A'hve never been here afore, Da.*

*Aye ye have, son.*

*When?*

*Ye'll no remember son, but this wis where you were first startit, in they big woods ower there.*

It wis true, ah mind that day fine, but imagine tellin a laddie of 16. He wis black affrontit, so he wis, and so wis ah.

Still they were good days then, ah wis mair spontaneous, no plannin everythin weeks in advance, while bein wi me cooled doon some of Jimmy's wilder schemes.

*It's a dead cert, hen, Boabby's pal knows the trainer.*

*Aw aye, and if you pit a week's wages on and loss it, whit dae we dae then?*

*We'll no loss it, it's a dead cert.*

*Jimmy . . .*

He knew the ice in that voice.

*A fiver then, doll.*

*A fiver wis a lot of money in they days.*

*A fiver . . .*

In the end ah got him doon tae ten boab each way.

And efter the hard times in the beginnin when Jimmy wis in and ooty jobs, things got easier and we hud wer weans and even startit tae go a holiday every year. And don't get me wrang, ah've never loved anybody else, but somewhere alang the line, well, ah lost ma relish fur him. It wis like when the doctor tellt me tae cut oot salt for ma blood pressure, food didnae taste the same. It wis the same food but it had lost its edge somehow, ah wis jist eatin it tae keep alive, no fur enjoyment.

Ah think it startit efter wee Jimmy wis born, the youngest, bitty an efterthought, ten year younger than Katie. Ah jist couldnae get on ma feet and then ah hud tae huv the operation. Well, the doctor said there wis nae point, ah widnae be wantin any mair weans and if it wis causin me grief . . . but ah never felt the same efter. Ah put on weight and, ah don't know whit it wis, but if ye don't feel like it, ah mean it's no like eatin, ye don't have tae dae it tae keep alive, dae ye? So insteidy him heatin me up, ma cauld somehow formed a glaister of frost ower the pair of us.

These folk that talk aboot the happy medium have got it all wrang. Life has its extremes, whether it's winnin the lottery or lossin yer faimly in a car crash, but they're no the hard part. It's the rest of it. Ah mind when ah wis a wee lassie and the teacher made us pit wan haun under the hot tap and wan under the cauld for a minute, then the baith of them intae a bowl of lukewarm watter, and of course the haun that wis hot felt cauld and the haun that wis cauld felt hot. But really, they were baith lukewarm and who ever wants anythin lukewarm? Ah wanted tae please Jimmy but it wis never the same and sometimes ah'd catch him lookin at me wi a sad puzzled look, a bit lik oor auld dug when she hud that medicine fae the vet.

We'd aye gone tae bed at the same time (ah let him get in five minutes early tae warm it up, right enough) but noo ah fund masel kiddin on ah wis glued tae some stupit TV programme.

*Early night the night, hen?*

*Ah'll no be long.*

*Naw?*

*Ah'll just watch the endy this furst.*

*Awright, hen.*

Jeezo, things are bad when ye turn doon a wee cuddle wi yer man fur an episode a *Prisoner Cell Block H*.

But tonight ah don't even pretend tae be watchin. Ah sit by the dyin fire, chitterin, cradlin the wee gless ball in ma hauns, transferrin it fae wan tae the other, watchin the white flakes drift roon the red rose. And ah know this is no light skimmer a snaw, this is a ringin frost. Ah pit ma haun on ma belly, doon below, a few inches tae the right, and ah feel it, ice crystals layer upon layer, growin inside me. Ah can see it in ma mind, like the big gless ball that we danced under when we were young, made up of a million glintin fragments, frozened tears. Ah know ah should of went tae the doctor's earlier, but somehow when you're used tae roukie weather you never notice the first flichters a snaw until it's too late and the world's a white wilderness.

Ah've tae go tae the hospital first thing the morra, though ah could tell fae the look on the doctor's face that there's no much they can do. Only the heat of the sun can melt the snaw and bring the earth back tae life and it's too late for that noo. Ah enter the daurk bedroom and creep between the sheets, fittin ma body snug in behind his back, ma face at his neck, knees tucked tight behind his. The contrast in temperature is almost too much for me at first, ah tingle as if ah have pins and needles, but efter a few minutes begin tae thaw.

*Jimmy.*

Ma breath kittles his neck and he wakes up wi a stert.

*Whit is it, hen?*

*Ah've got somethin tae tell you.*

*Aye, lass.*

He turns ower, pits his airms roon me and pulls me close tae his bosie. Ah coorie intae the warmth, feelin his big hert pulsin under his chest.

# A CHANGE OF HERT

It was the ice-cream. That's how ah knew. He's never in his life eaten chocolate ice-cream, never really liked ice-cream at all, maybe take a cone or a wee drop vanilla if it's really hot, but tae see him shovellin rich dark chocolate ice-cream intae his mooth. Ah never said anythin but. After all, it's a big operation, he's bound tae be different. The doctor had warned us he'd maybe even be a bit depressed or that.

Then he started gaun tae the park, just sittin, lookin at the floral displays. No that there's any herm in that, but if you'd knew him afore. The only thing he'd spend hours lookin at wis the racin on the TV. To tell the truth it made me nervous. It's nice tae sit and look at flooers for five minutes but efter that ah start wantin tae dae sumpn, go the messages, dae a washin. Ah didnae want tae say anythin for ah wis feart ah'd upset him, so ah went tae the doctor, the young wan wi the fair hair.

*It's aboot Peter, doctor, ah'm worried aboot him.*

*I don't think you've any need to worry, Mrs Cameron. Your husband's making very good progress. It'll take a while – after all, a heart transplant's a big operation – but by and large we're very pleased with him. Was there anything in particular you were worried about?*

*No, doctor, it's no that, it's just, well, he's no hissel any mair.*

He leaned forward in his seat. His glasses slid doon his nose and he pushed them back.

*You know, after this type of surgery it's quite normal for patients to be depressed or experience mood swings that are totally out of character.*

*But it's no that, it's the ice-cream.*

*Ice-cream?*

*He never ate chocolate ice-cream afore, and he doesnae watch the racin any mair. He sits in the park and when he's sleepin he lies on his left side.*

He ran his haun through his hair, pushin it back aff his foreheid.

*When you've been merriet for 30 year, you know which side he sleeps on, and he aye slept on the right afore.*

*Mrs Cameron, I'm aware you've been under a lot of stress recently.*

*Doctor, whose hert did he get?*

*You know that the donor was a young woman who'd been involved in a car crash. I can't tell you any more than that.*

*Ah know, but who was she, what was she like? Did she eat chocolate ice-cream?*

He cleared his throat and put his haun ower his mooth. Ah knew he wis tryin no tae laugh.

*Look, the heart is just a pump, a big muscle. There's no way that getting someone else's heart could make your husband like or dislike the things they did.*

*OK, doctor.*

*I think, though, that you're needing a good rest. I'll arrange for Peter to go into respite care for a few days and you go away for a break. Go and visit your daughter. It would do you good.*

*Ah'll think aboot it.*

*Come back and see me again if you're still worried, but really, everything's fine.*

Ah stopped at the chapel on ma way hame. It's no like me, ah'm no very religious really, but sometimes that cool darkness helps calm me doon.

There's an atmosphere in a chapel, some would cry it the presence of God and maybe it is, or maybe it's just that hunners and thoosands of folk have prayed and hoped and sat quiet among the marble and the statues. Ah lit a caunle in fronty the Sacred Hert statue an knelt doon. The tremblin light threw shadows roon the alcove and the statue stood oot sharp in front. Ah felt as though ah'd never really looked at it properly afore, never seen how strange it wis; Jesus, wan haun raised in blessin, the other pointin at his hert, red and open on his chist. The nuns tellt us it was a symbol of his love for the world. He wore his hert on the ootside because his love was that big it wis for everybody, while ordinary folk had theirs on the inside, for our love wis just human.

It wis all very well that doctor tellin me the hert's just a pump, but that's no how it feels. So ah believed in ma heid whit the doctor said, but ah knew in ma hert that ma Peter wisnae the same man as afore the operation. Ah knew the doctor widnae tell me ony mair, it wis supposed tae be confidential. A young woman who'd died in a car crash. Ah widnae even have known that much, but the nurse let it slip oot. Ah had tae find oot mair aboot her.

The Mitchell Library's a beautiful buildin. No a very nice settin since they stuck that motorway right through in fronty it, but the buildin sits grand an dignified, aw lit up at night too. You think you're really gaun somewhere when you walk up they stairs and through the polished widden doors. The big brass haunles have the Glesga coat of airms on them, though the left wan has been rubbed that hard it's nearly flat. Funny that, you'd think the right wan wid be mair worn. Course then ah discover ah should of went in the side entrance and ah had tae deposit ma bag and get a ticket and a crumpled poly bag tae pit ma stuff in, but at last ah fund masel in the Glesga Room, where they keep the newspapers. Ah thought ah'd be lookin through piles of them, but they have them on microfilm noo, so you read them on a screen like a giant TV. Ah cawed the haunle roon an roon, checkin each page. Mair'n likely she'd have died in the area, because they didnae like tae move the hert too far. Ah thought it would take ages but ah'd been at it less than twenty minutes afore the words seemed tae jump oot at me fae *The Herald*, January 14th. It was a paragraph in wee print stuck doon the side of a page headed 'News in Brief'.

'Late last night, Fiona Macintosh, 27, a nurse from Greenock, was killed when her car went out of control and crashed. It is believed that the car hit a patch of black ice. No other vehicles were involved and there were no witnesses. Mrs Macintosh is survived by her husband Thomas, 31. She was expecting her first child at the time of the accident.'

Ah sat listenin tae the hum of the machine, starin at the letters on the screen but no longer readin them. The excitement ah'd felt drained away and ah was seized by a creepin cauld. Ah kept seein this lassie, on her way hame fae her work likely, and that moment when she realises her car's oot of control. Ah hope she didnae know, ah hope tae God she wisnae conscious for long, thinkin aboot her wee bairn an the life ebbin oot the two of them.

*Excuse me, are you all right?*

The young lassie that showed me how tae find the newspaper stories wis staunin beside the desk.

*You look as if you've had a shock. Are you all right?*

*Ah've had a bit of a shock, hen, but ah'm OK.*

Ma hauns were freezin.

*A wee cup of tea would help, ah think.*

*There's a tearoom downstairs, I'll take you down in the lift.*

*Thanks, hen.*

Sittin at the Formica table, ah felt ma hauns warmin in the heat of the cup, tinglin as the numbness wore aff. There ah wis, thinkin ah'd find oot mair aboot the lassie, maybe write tae her faimly or even just go tae her hoose and look at it fae the ootside, try tae get some sense of her. It had seemed that important tae know mair aboot her, if she liked gairdens, if she ate ice-cream.

But how could ah dae that noo, efter whit ah'd read. All ah could think aboot wis her man, waitin for her tae come hame, startin tae worry she wis late, mibbae lookin oot at the weather, thinkin aboot an accident, but no really believin it, then the polis arrivin at the door and – everythin stops. Just aboot the same time as we're gettin the phone call fae the hospital.

*We think we have found a donor for you.*

Nae wonder Peter's no hissel, nae wonder he's quiet and wants tae sit in the park and watch flooers. Sumbdy died and gied him their hert. Ah make ma way oot the library across tae the bridge, high above the motorway where the traffic roars by like a big river. Ah staund in the drizzlin mist, haud tight tae the metal palins, watch cars follow triangles of dirty light.

# DINDY

Dindy dindy dindy says Tommam.
    Bingy bingy bingy.

I can hear that rustlin in there. Rustle rustle rustle, yez are always at it. Under the covers and all. There's a blue packet on that table, it's tea biscuits, I can smell them.

*And he left him there, just left him there without a thought. Went off to have a drink, sit in the sun. I thought he'd be safe there, he says. After all, it was supposed to be a playgroup or something, crèche thingy, they said, for the weans.*
    *Blamin me.*
    *He says, but you said to take him, he'd enjoy it. Yes, yes, but not to leave him there hissel, I never thought ye'd leave him there an fuck off. I'm sorry and he was all right, wasn't he, he was all right.*
    *I was only doing a bit of shopping.*

Humpo humpo.
    I need a fuck. A good fuck would sort me out, all these twitches and shivers in my bones. But there's no use in hopin and wasting your life away. Take what you git. They're all the same, men, anyway, there's not one of them's worth the heat in his drawers.

*Eventually, aye, he was eventually, when he'd calmed down, still clingin tae his mammy for a good while after though, still coories in, arms round ma neck like a wee limpet. No like him at all either, him so independent.*

It's the wee red boots, sittin there neatly beside the chair. The owld chair with the stuffing comin out, the one that's in the kitchen for when he's playin around, spilling things an gettin crumbs ower everything. Wee red boots with a zip and laces, wee red boots that could of been made by the shoemaker or the elves in the story, his mammy's favourite when she was wee.

*It was the panic, but, the way it rose and took me over when I thought he was lost, frantic runnin round that place, shouting his name, crawlin under stuff, owld boxes and furniture and all that crap was lyin round on the upper floors, and why the hell would they leave stuff like that lyin round when they were supposed tae be runnin a crèche, for God's sake, why the hell were they allowed to, that fuckin festival gets away with murder, that wumman so calm and as if she didn't care, he'd be there somewhere.*

Conky conky noondoo noondoo
No even a cup of tea, no even a sip of tea to slake the drouth.
Nimble nimble nimble. Slake slake slake. And when she pauses for a moment
flakety flakety flake.

*Aye, somewhere lyin under a pile a rubble with his leg trapped, somewhere in a dark corner feart, feart cos his daddy's no more sense than he was born with and the authorities let stupit women like that run*

*fuckin crèches in the middle of unsuitable buildins.*
   *Mammy, can you watch him the morra?*


The wee red boots waiting for him to wake up get up into the world.
Those boots say, Aye, it's me, here I am. He knows who he is. He has a
name he is Tommam. TommAM.
   It's too EARLY.
   I don't want to get up I don't want to I want to sleep then get up late
and sit in the sunshine with a croissant in a café.


   I have a little pony her name is dapple grey.
   What's that?
   It's yer granny's blouse.
   What's that?
   It's yer granny's blouse.
   No Iggy Pop then?


   Giggle giggle giggle
   Chuckle chuckle chuckle.
   By the hair on my chinny chin chin
   I will not let you in.


   No never never never yes'll no get me. Yes'll no find me, no matter
where yez look.


   Knock knock
   Who's there?
   It's the big bad wolf.
   What does he want?
   Want a cup of tea.

Yer granny'll put the kettle on.

It's the only way to get a cup of tea round here. Put the kettle on yerself. Shrivel away intae a dried up bit of stick afore she'll make you a cup of tea. She'll hardly bother tae lift the rubbish off the chair tae let ye sit down.

Polly put the kettle on
Polly put the kettle on

*What does he want. I mean, what does he want from me? I mean, when he was here, he never paid any attention to me, he never even looked at me when he was talking to me. And as for the wee one, well, it's no as if he was a bad father to him. No, I'm no saying that, but it's just, he's like a wean hissel, he's no sense. He comes in here after his work, after the pub, no late or that, just a few drinks, but I've got the wean intae his jammies, readin a story, nice and quiet and what does he do?*

What does he do?

*He starts chuckin him up and down in the air, liftin him up high ower his shoulders, high in the air and the wee fella's laughing and gigglin and laughing and gigglin.*

Hahaha

Heeheehee

Gosh, Granny! Gosh!

That's a funny word.

Hahahaheeheehee.

Surely, surely.

They're all the same, men.

*And it's no him that has tae get him tae sleep after.*

*

The leaves are turning. Green turning green turning gold turning red turning russet turning rustle rustle russstle underfoot.

It's the wee red wellies lying under the table, waiting for him tae go out and splash in the puddles. He can put them on hissel. Tuck the wee breeks in.

Splash! SSPLASH!

What's that?

It's leaves.

Leafs.

Splash in the leafs.


here we go round the mulberry bush, the mulberrry bush the mulberry bush


What the fuck's a mulberry bush? Where does all this crap come from? Bloody *Listen with Mother* every day at two o clock. Never missed it, her and her sisters. Sitting on the settee in a row, squashed in the five of them. How the hell did five of them get ontae that owld couch? Fifteen minutes of peace and quiet for me tae get a fag in the kitchen.

*I wish you wouldn't smoke in front of that wean, Mammy.*

But there couldn't of been five of them at the one time though, they wouldn't of all been at home at the one time, some of them would of been at school surely.

Surely, surely.

In the holidays, right enough.

Christmas holidays, making dinners and sandwiches and dinners and sandwiches and hot drinks for the ones with colds. Summer holidays, making their clothes for the new term and sandwiches for the park and bandaging the skint knees. Plaits. Plaiting each other's hair and putting the elastic bands at the ends and the ribbons tied over the top. Tartan ribbons.

The sky's darkening now, lowering. It's gonnae rain, it'll pour soon.

In the mall it's a glittering palace, a fairy-tale world. We can sit in the café, watch the buses stop at the stop, unload and load their passengers, move on.

Sing tinkle star, Granny.

No in the café.

Sing it!

And the flowers are curled like tissue paper, rustle like tissue paper, lemon tulips, pink and purple ones, dry like talcum next your cheeks. Wafer-thin paper furled round a black stalk. He's lifted one out and he's running away with it.

You'll get lifted!

Lifted by the polis.

The big polis man'll get you.

*Don't, Mammy, don't make him feart of the polis.*

Another cup of coffee, another.

And the grey skies drift dark rainclouds.

He had a raincoat. A gaberdine one that belted round him. Men don't wear raincoats now, nobody does, it's anoraks, but they don't call them that either. I don't know what they call them now. And the old men wear them too but they're neat and beige-looking. Zips up the front. I wouldn't even know him now if I saw him, he'd be wearing an anorak with a zip up it. Walking about the mall. Maybe he'd have no hair now. On his head anyway. Grey pubes. Pubes. That's what they call them now. We never called them anything. But I like that word. Shut yer pubes. Wash yer pubes. Get off yer pubes. Sook my pubes. Some chance.

*Sorry I'm late, there was a rush at the last minute. Where is he?*

He's all right, he's.

*Mammy, don't let him play there, it's dangerous, it's too slippy, he could fall.*

Oh he could, so he could.

*How's my boy?*

Oh, he's fine, survived another day dicing with death with auld Grannygreypubes.

Sing tinkle star, Mammy.

*No in the café.*

Sing it!

Home again home again jiggety jog

What's for tea?

Mince and tatties.

No want.

Carrots and dumplings.

No want.

The rest of them loved my soup. She always made a face, said it made her feel sick to look at the bits of barley. He grabbed her by her hair shoved her face into the soup, yanked it back up again, the tartan ribbon soggy and dreepin down the side of her face.

The only time he done anything like it right enough, he had his reasons. It wasn't her that riled him, she just got in the way, her and her faces. Lady Muck he called her. Don't turn yer nose up at good food. Barley snotterin off the ends of her nose.

Eat my bogies.

Bogie had a gaberdine raincoat. I never liked him, Humphrey Bogart. I'd rather of humped Clark Gable or whatsisface Cary. Cary Grant. He'd never of worn an anorak. Beautiful overcoats he had, perfect cut. And his hair. Lovely shiny hair, probably got a hairdresser to cut his pubes for him.

Just a trim old boy.

Watch those scissors don't get too close to my wee man.


Curly wurly. A finger of.


*I don't know why he's so fussy about his food. Has he been eating rubbish this afternoon, Mammy?*

I say, old girl, this is a bloody good dustbin for a snackette of an afternoon. Vol-au-vents a speciality. Don't spare the ribs, what?


Here's yer lovely mince.

No want.

You need to eat.

No want.

If you don't eat you won't grow up to be a big strong boy.

*He was never fussy about his food before.*

We were never fussy about our food. Rationing. If you don't get enough, you appreciate it all the more.


And we never did get enough, did we?


*No you can't have chips. I'm telling you, it's him, he's no more sense than . . . he takes him out and gives him chips. Chips, chips, chips every time. So I'm the big baddy when I try to get him to eat a decent meal.*


Knock knock.

Who's there?

It's the big bad wolf.

What does he want?

Chips.

Salt and vinegar, batter sticking to the paper, steam rising into the cold air just round the corner in the back lane oh oh oh.

You'll have had your

chips.

Smack your lips, sook on it, roll yer tongue round it, slurp slurp.

Rustle rustle rustle.

What's that?

Well, we don't want any wee accidents do we? Any wee buns in the ovens when the baker comes home.

No, we just want chips.


Mmm mmm mmm

Yum yumyum

This is yummy, Mammy.

That's a funny word.

Gosh, Granny, gosh!

Hahhahhahhahhah ahah ah ah ohohohoh oh.


Want to play with my ball before my bed.

I'll bet you do, son.

Play with the balls, the wee bouncy balls jiggling around in yer hand, bouncing around against yer bum, bouncy bounce, afore ye come. A finger of fuck is just enough to give your girl a treat.


It's been a long time coming. All these twitches and shivers.

*At least he's no coming round the night at least. At least I'll be able to get him tae his bed at a decent hour. I mean he's a good daddy, he is a good daddy, I'll give him that, it's just. I mean I never thought I'd end up like this. Oh well, it could be worse.*

*He's a good daddy, really.*

He is really.

*Just a big wean.*

They're all the same, men. Take what ye git.


Where's my daddy?

He's at the footie the night, son. You'll see him the morra.

*I mean, weans need their daddys, they need their daddys, they do. I mean, look at me and my daddy, I was always a daddy's girl.*

You were.

*Even looked just like him.*

His pet.

*Dark hair, very dark.*

Dark, always very dark.

Rustle rustle rustle.

Everything rustled then, now it's all zips and Velcro, scrapes and scratches.

Cannae see a fuckin thing in this dark.

Night night, Granny, night night, Mammy.

To feel his arms round me, to feel his heart beat.

Night night, gie's a kiss afore ye go.

Yes, please.


Knock knock

Who's there?

It's the big bad wolf?

I'm feart.

Knock knock, yes please, knock knock, knock knees. You never see anybody with knock knees now. Used tae be every other wifie on the street was shaughlin along the road bowly as a banana, pleasure bent he always cried it, handy for if ye were at it standing up. Oh well, it was a long time ago now, what's the difference. There's no difference, they're all the same, treated them all the same, never made any difference. Five of them sitting on the settee in a row, squashed in the five of them.

*Don't sit on that owld settee, Mammy, it's just in here for when he's playing about and it doesn't matter.*

It doesn't matter.

They all had tartan ribbons. Drippin down the side of her face the soup. The only time.

Cold air dry like talcum. The only time.

# LOAST

It's thon tree ootside the bedroom windae; overhangin branches fill the sky, big black burds nest in it, swoopin by lik enemy planes. It waves in the wind and muddies the light and things move aboot. You put them in the drawer an they turn up in the wardrobe, so you blame Agnes; it must be her, there's naebdy else here, but she says *it wisnae me* and gies you wanny her looks that makes you want tae greet. Words, too, keep gettin loast inside yer heid somewhere. You're lookin at sumpn that you know the word for and you're rummlin aboot inside yer heid, inside aw that cottonwool stuff that seems tae float aboot inside yer heid nooadays, but you canny fun it. Somebdy's moved that too. Your words trail aff then you clear your throat an say, *thingummy* or *ye know*, lik an ordinary person that's jist forgotten a word fur a minute. So they try tae guess the word and you say *that's it*, even if it's no, jist so's you can finish the sentence. And you wish you'd never said anythin in the furst place, and mibbe next time you'll no bother.

Maisty the time you don't need tae bother anyway, there's just you and Agnes and you havenae much to say tae each other after aw these years. She never had any patience wi your conversation even before the words started tae get loast in your heid, she'd raither have read a book or sumpn than listen tae you jabberin oan lik a daft wee burdie. Folk think, because you're sisters and you live thegither, you must be close; even send postcards tae The Misses O'Halloran, as if you were a married couple. Or A&B O'Halloran, like a firm of lawyers. She hates that, thinks it's disrespectful no tae put the proper titles on. She used tae work in an office so she knows what's correct. You don't care, just wish somebdy'd send one addressed to you on your ain, so you could put it on the dressin table in your room, look at it in the mornin when you wake up.

You were never close that way wi Agnes, no even when you were young and you all ran aboot thegither. But it didnae matter then, for you'd your work to go tae, you loved the shop wi its wooden cabinets full of beautiful sweaters, fingerin the Cashmere and angora as you spread them oot for the customer. *Yes sir, she'll love that. It'll wash beautifully, madam. Perfect with your colourin.* And your bletherin was a gift then, the customers came back time and again, you made them feel special, remembered all their names. And after your work you went oot wi your pals, and Jean and her man came visitin wi the nieces and nephews; then away a sudden it seemed tae be you and Agnes, on your ain, no really likin each ither that much, jist here thegither like two auld bits a leftower furniture.

And you hate this hoose but you cannae get away fae it because she won't let you; you've hated it for years wi its cauld rooms and ugly wallpaper and uncomfortable chairs, but she'll no move. She likes bein uncomfortable. She'll no admit it but she does, always sits in the hardest chair at the most awkward angle for the TV, so she has tae peer roond wi her heid tae wan side. Puts the dishes up high where she has tae climb up tae them. *That's where they've always been*, she says when Jean asks why she doesnae move them nearer. You thought you might of moved in wi Jean after her man passed on, thought she'd be glad of your company now the weans are grown up and oot the hoose, but she didnae take the hint, so you're stuck wi Agnes. You depend on her noo, you cannae dae things on your ain any mair, lik go the messages or take the bus intae toon, because you keep lossin things. You've loast the words tae say tae the bus driver and you get mixed up wi the money; it looks like bits a paper to you, funny wee scrumply bits a paper in your purse. Sometimes you feel lik takin it oot an throwin it roon the place, lettin it fly in every direction lik pee-the-beds blown by the wind, for whit use is it to you noo? You cannae buy anythin you want wi it any mair, because there is nothin you want. All you want is to get back tae bein yoursel, an you know that money cannae dae that.

It's funny when you think of how important it used tae be to you, that money at the endy the week in a wee broon envelope. You felt lik a millionaire gaun tae the shops and buying sumpn tae wear fur the dancin or jist sittin in the café, drinkin coffee an watchin folk walk aboot the street. For you were aye turned oot lovely in thae days, everybdy said so; you loved bright colours lik yella an red an emerald green an you had everythin matchin, bags an shoes and beads. When there was nights oot you aye hud the nicest rigoot. You used tae make yer ain claes tae; your fingers were that neat and clever, whizzin alang on that old black Singer machine.

But noo you look in the mirror and you cannae see yoursel any mair, jist a wee loast shape, faded away in the distance, the mirror misty and milky as though somebdy hus smeared it wi poalish and forgotten tae rub it aff. And you cannae really be boathered wi your body any mair, disnae seem lik your body, it's hardly worth the trouble of gettin it washed and dressed, for who sees you noo anyway, except if you huv tae go tae the doactor.

You like gaun tae the doactor an you spend a loaty time gettin ready fur him; havin a bath, even puttin on powder and lipstick. It's the prepa-ration you like best really, to have sumpn tae prepare fur. And you like sittin in the waitin room, watchin the other patients, for they smile at you, but usually they don't talk or, if they dae, it's no difficult, no a real conversation that you huv tae answer. *No as cauld the day. Naw. It's that wee wumman doacter that's oan. Oh aye.* It's enough tae nod and smile and you can still do that right enough, even you. Sometimes there's weans in the waitin room and you've aye liked weans, especially wee lassies; you like their soft hair an the nice colours they wear. Even though they don't wear frocks nooadays, they're still lovely. They remind you of your nieces when they were wee, when you used tae buy them things, then sometimes they stayed ower at the weekend, and you would watch them sleepin, breathin that deep as only weans kin. Sometimes you'd imagine they were your weans, sing a lullaby, strokin their fingers as they slept. It never seemed fair, Jean havin five when you never even had one. Just wan wee lassie. She'd of had fair curly hair and a blue coat wi a velvet collar. Black patent shoes and white socks, soft pink knees. You'd of tied her hair wi a red ribbon, brushin it oot every night afore the fire, read her a story and, when she got aulder, you'd of done things thegither, in the toon. You used tae go intae toon wi Helen right enough. Once when you were buyin her a special frock for a party, the assistant thoat she wis your daughter and she said, *Oh, she's no ma mammy, she's my auntie,* and you felt hurt for a minute, but she was only tellin the truth after aw.

It's no the same though, havin a niece insteidy a daughter, fur a daughter would visit you every week, no wanst every few months lik Helen. A daughter would come tae the doactor's wi you an explain things tae him, a daughter wouldnae let you go on your ain an get all mixed up wi your words tae you burst oot greetin. A daughter would make them do sumpn aboot it insteidy gieing you pink and yella pills that you forget tae take and you don't know whit they're fur anyhow. A daughter would dae that.

A daughter would be saft wi you, no hard an fierce lik a sister. She's so hard on you noo, you don't remember her bein so hard on you before.

Sometimes you look at her hunched over the newspaper and see a big black crow, pointy and jaggy, and wonder whit happened tae the sister you used tae go dancin wi, gigglin ower the sodjers thegither. Thae boys, hunners of them there wis, brave and smart in their khaki, but they got loast tae, they never came back then efter the war, there werenae enough to go roon, an there were three sisters; you couldnae expect them aw tae get men. Jean wis the wan that goat a man; a good man, hud tae be a man for yous aw, fixin things roon the hoose lik a man dis, quiet wi calm, steady hauns.

If he wis here that tree would never huv grown sae high, bloackin oot the light. He would huv cut thae branches back an you wouldnae keep lossin things in this room, but noo you huv tae get workmen in and she disnae like payin for anythin an the cooncil are that slow. There was that tap that kept drippin aw night; it wis that loud, you thoat it hud got oot the bathroom and moved inside yer heid, but it's sorted noo. They're comin the day, the men, tae fix the tree, and when aw the branches are cut aff, the light will come intae this room again and these shadows will go. Mibbe then you'll stop lossin things.

# ZIMMEROBICS

A self-contained flat; one bedroom, security entrance and a view of the communal garden. A lovely house, with its fresh white walls and a green swirly-patterned carpet that doesn't show the dirt. Catherine, my niece, went to a lot of trouble to do it up.

'Better than where you were. You had no view there. You're so lucky.'

I know I'm lucky and I didn't mean to be ungrateful. It's just that a sheltered house meant the end of everything. This was it, this view, for the rest of my life.

It's not really a life anyone would choose, getting old. Things don't work properly any more, not so badly that I'm helpless, just enough to be annoying. I can walk with a Zimmer but it's so much trouble to shove the thing in front of me that most of the time I can't be bothered. Stupid name, Zimmer. Why is it called that? Zimmer is German for room but it can't be that. Maybe it's the noise it makes as you shuffle along with it – zim, zim, zim.

And there's this constant feeling of awareness in every part of my body; jaggy pains in my elbows and knees, vertebrae grinding against one another, bits that used to fit together smoothly now clicking and crunking like the central-heating boiler starting up. I did once try to explain it to Catherine.

'It's like the shows, those games where you get a circle on a stick and you have to feed it along a piece of twisted wire, very carefully without touching it and, if you touch the wire a bell rings.'

'Uh-huh.' She is busy rearranging ornaments on the mantlepiece.

'It's like that. I have to do everything really slowly and carefully, otherwise it hurts.'

Catherine gave me one of her looks and said I should take more interest in things. She knows I can't knit any more and reading tires me but she's always trying to get me to put photographs in albums or watch the TV.

'*Top Hat*'s on TV this afternoon,' she said as she was getting ready to leave. 'Fred Astaire and Ginger Rogers.'

'Oh, is it?'

'It starts at two-thirty and it's all set for you. I'm away for the two o'clock bus. See you on Friday.'

I didn't watch the film. I'd rather sit and daydream out of the window, lost inside my own head. Catherine can't understand as it's not in her nature to daydream or dawdle or drift. She's like an office stapler, precisely snapping shut, securing papers in the correct order forever. She never lets anything go. When she returned on Friday the first thing she said to me was:

'Did you enjoy the film?'

I was caught off my guard.

'The film?'

'*Top Hat* – you didn't watch it, did you? I knew you wouldn't. I don't know why I bother. You've no interest in anything outside yourself. You never even bother to go along to the dayroom. There's three ladies sitting there now, having a wee chat. You could go and meet people.'

Catherine always pronounces 'meet' as if it were printed in capital letters. This was one of her favourite monologues, that I should MEET people in the dayroom. I knew I could shuffle along there with my

Zimmer but I could never be bothered. There was bingo on Mondays and a drink on Saturday nights but I never went to either. She thinks I'm a snob, that I think I'm better than these women but it's not that; it's just. I'd rather sit here.

She likes to get away sharp on a Friday because the traffic's busier and the buses take longer. She set the TV up and left me with the remote control on my lap.

'Here you are. You're so lucky. I wish I could sit down and watch a film.'

I refrained from saying there was nothing to stop her from watching the film if she chose. All her busy-ness is self-inflicted. Not that I don't appreciate her. I do. She visits me twice a week, on Tuesdays and Fridays, and always brings something home-cooked, like mince and potatoes or apple pie; much nicer than the meals the home help makes. I just wish she'd sit down and talk to me instead of rushing round the house tidying my clothes and checking inside the wardrobe to see if I've hung up my skirt.

'I tidied out those drawers last Friday and now look at them. This sweater was in with your stockings!'

I don't know why it makes a difference to her whether my drawers are tidy or not. I don't care so why should she?

I waited till I heard her footsteps disappear along the corridor, then I switched it off. I can't be bothered with TV. The picture is sharp and bright with no fuzziness round the edges. I prefer to watch things that are faded like the bush outside the window. It's starting to put out its shoots after the winter and when the sun comes out it sparkles in a copper haze.

I gazed out of the window. It was dull and the bush looked grey.

'Hello. Anybody in?' A voice called from the door.

Its owner was tall and slim, with long auburn hair, the colour that mine used to be when I was young. Her smile had lots of even white teeth, the kind you usually see on Americans but, when she spoke, she was obviously a local girl.

'Hi there. Mrs Knight?'

'Miss Knight.'

'Miss Knight. I'm Cheryl.'

'How do you do?'

I supposed she must be another one of these women who come to visit me for a variety of reasons I can't be bothered to remember. They think you get confused but I don't. It just doesn't matter to me whether they're the social worker, the home-help coordinator, the district nurse or whatever. The only one that's any different is the hairdresser. At least she does something useful while she's here. I like getting my hair washed and set. I specially like it when she puts me under that drier thing and I shut my eyes while the warm air flows round my head and the drone of the machine makes me drift off into a doze.

Cheryl perched on the arm of the chair opposite me.

'I'm here to tell you about the exercise sessions we're starting in the dayroom next week.'

'Oh.'

'They're specially designed for senior citizens like yourself, gentle exercises to help increase your mobility and get your body working a bit better.'

She sounded as if she'd learned it off by heart.

'Oh.'

'Do you do any exercises just now?'

I looked down at my legs and waved my arm vaguely.

'Well, no, dear, I can't really move about much.'

'They'll be just the thing for you.'

'But I couldn't do anything like that – you see I walk with a Zimmer.'

'That's OK. Most of the residents use a Zimmer. The exercises are specially designed for people with Zimmers; in fact, I'm thinking of calling the class Zimmerobics.'

'You are?'

'I try to do that with all my classes. Give them snappy titles.'

She sat down properly on the chair and continued in a more confidential tone.

'It's easy to get classes in the evenings because that's when working people want to do them, but during the day it's a bit harder. So I've tried to go for different markets. I do a class on a Tuesday for mums with young babies – the babies take part.'

'The babies do aerobics? How advanced they are nowadays.'

She smiled.

'They don't exactly do aerobics; the mums lift them and use them as part of their routine, a bit like lifting weights. The babies love it. I call that class Baberobics.'

She paused, waiting, I presumed, for me to say something. I couldn't think of a reply but nodded my head in what I hoped was an encouraging manner. She continued.

'So now I'm targeting older people. If it's a success, I'm hoping to get a business grant. There's lots of old folk's homes looking for something like this for their residents. I really want to make a video and sell it so that all up and down the country there are senior citizens doing Zimmerobics with Cheryl.'

'Well, dear, that sounds very nice. I hope you're successful.'

'So I'll see you on Thursday then? Eleven o'clock.'

'I'll think about it.'

That's what I always say when I've no intention of doing something but, over the weekend, I kept thinking about it. I'd seen aerobics on the TV once when I'd lost the remote control and couldn't switch the thing

off; impossibly shaped women in shiny skin-tight clothes doing things
with their bodies I didn't know bodies did. The idea of Cheryl teaching
that sort of thing to us; humphy-backit, shuffling behind metal frames
with our swollen feet, well, it didn't bear thinking about. There was
something about the girl, though, her enthusiasm about the project, that
attracted me. I've always been attracted by enthusiasts, not being one
myself.

Anyway I should have known Catherine would make me go.

'I hope you've signed up for these exercise classes,' she said as she
swept into the room on Tuesday.

'I'm not sure if it would be good for me, dear. At my age you have to
be careful about exercise.'

'Careful! You hardly move from your chair except to go to the toilet.
Anyway I phoned the doctor and she said there was no reason why you
shouldn't do gentle exercises. In fact, she said it would do you good.'


So that was that. At 11 am I assembled with the others in the dayroom. I
knew most of their faces, but was surprised to see some of them wearing
tracksuits and trainers. It hadn't occurred to me to ask what to wear and
I didn't possess such things anyway, but somehow I felt out of place. It
was like starting school and discovering that the others were wearing
school uniform and you weren't.

Cheryl bounced into the room, wearing a pair of trainers that made
her feet look like a horse's hooves. Her hair was tied back with an
emerald green band which matched her shimmering leotard and tights.

'I hope she doesn't need to go to the toilet in a hurry,' muttered a voice
behind me.

'Hi there. It's great to see so many of you here this morning. Now,
take it at your own pace and if you feel uncomfortable or out of breath
any time, stop for a wee rest. Enjoy!'

She switched on the music. We stood behind our Zimmers as she got us to stretch first one, then the other, arm, move our heads to each side, then stretch our legs. I heard a few creaking sounds but so far so good. We moved on to circling movements and, as the record progressed, I felt an unaccustomed but pleasant tingling in my limbs.

'That was the warm-up. The next one's a bit faster.'

The next record was a catchy tune about living in the YMCA. I couldn't keep up with the routine at first but, once we'd been through it a few times, I became quite proficient. We had to raise our right then our left arms to the Y and the M, then pause on the C and hold our Zimmers as we bent both legs for the A. Then we marched (well, shuffled in most cases) round to the left, raised our left arms twice to the Y and the M (that was a bit tricky), paused at the C and kicked our left leg out to the A. During the verse we did some marching and a few kicks, then we repeated the chorus routine, this time moving to the right. At the end we clapped three times, boldly taking both hands off our Zimmer frames.

It was brilliant. I hadn't felt like this for years. My body was old and decrepit, but it still worked. I had been concentrating so hard on what I was doing I had forgotten the others, but now I looked round and saw their faces, flushed and smiling.

'You all did great. Give yourselves a round of applause.' She clapped her hands above her head while we patted our hands together, slightly embarrassed.

'Same time next week,' she called as we hirpled out of the dayroom, old once again.

The memory of the exercise class lingered on for the rest of the day, not just in my mind as I relived the routine, but in my bones and muscles. I thought I'd be sore and stiff but, surprisingly, I felt better, as though someone had oiled all the creaky old joints. There was a feeling in them which I suppose you would call an ache, but it was a pleasant ache, an ache of life.

'Could you buy me a tracksuit?'

Catherine looked surprised. It's usually her suggesting that I need something like a new skirt or some underwear and me saying, 'Well, if you think so, dear'.

'A tracksuit?'

'Some of the others have got tracksuits. I thought it would be more comfortable.'

'They've got nice ones in Asda. I could get it along with the messages.'

'And trainers too?'

'Of course.'

'But don't put yourself to any bother.'

There's nothing she likes better than to be put to some bother.

'No bother at all,' she smiled. 'Told you you'd enjoy the class if you only made an effort.'

The tracksuit was emerald green, in a soft and fleecy material which stroked my skin as I moved, with no restricting straps or chafing seams. The trainers felt like balloons on my feet. I stretched and swayed through the warm-up, feeling graceful and light and, when the 'YMCA' music began, I was amazed to find my body somehow remembered what it had done last week without my having to think. In fact, I did stop to think about it at one point and that was the only time I made a mistake. I even found myself singing along to the chorus, though I couldn't make out most of the words.

'Well done, everyone. That was even better than last week. Give yourselves a round of applause.'

Cheryl looked at me and smiled. 'You certainly enjoyed yourself, Miss Knight.'

'I did, dear, very much.'

'And you've got all the gear now.'

'Pardon?'

'The tracksuit – it's lovely, really suits you.'

'Thank you, dear.'

Cheryl started running the classes twice a week, on Mondays as well as Thursdays, and the warden served tea afterwards. I was about to go off to my flat when Edna, a bony woman with watery grey eyes, touched my arm and said: 'I've been wondering where you got your tracksuit; it's such a lovely colour.'

'Oh, thank you.'

'It really suits you,' said another woman, whose navy-blue one definitely didn't suit her.

'Thank you. My niece got it for me.'

And somehow I became drawn into the conversation and it really wasn't that bad. In fact, I stayed behind after every class.

A few weeks later Cheryl announced she was going to make a video. I couldn't wait to tell Catherine.

'A video? What for?'

'I think it's so that other people can watch us and learn the exercises.'

'Aren't you glad I persuaded you to go to these classes?'

'Do you think you could get me a headband? Cheryl wears one, she pushes her hair back with it, like an Alice band.'

'And you want one?'

'For the video. I thought it would keep my hair off my face.'

I wasn't sure what making a video would entail but I expected it to be very complicated with teams of people putting up lights and make-up girls powdering our faces every five minutes. I thought we'd have to keep stopping and starting while they filmed but it wasn't like that at all, just two young men with tiny cameras that would have fitted into your handbag. Cheryl stood at the front of the class with only a slight quiver in her voice to show she was nervous.

'Just ignore the cameras. You all know the routine, you're brilliant, so do your best and put a bit of oomph into it.'

I felt a flutter in my heart and my knees trembled a bit; then the music started and I forgot everything else, moving inside myself as I always did during the exercises, aware of my breath quickening and my nerves and blood coming alive inside me. Then all of a sudden it was over. Everyone was smiling and talking and patting each other on the back but I felt like crying. I didn't want to talk to anybody. I didn't want to stay for the cup of tea.

I slipped away and returned to my flat, holding tight to the handrail which stretched the length of the corridor. It was a filthy day outside and the room was full of shadows. I sat in my chair looking out at the bush, its leaves washed with grey, feeling the joints at the top of my legs easing, warmth seeping down. It felt very strange, as though my body was heavy and light at the same time, floating above the chair yet fixed to it. The sky darkened to near black and the rain started, soft rain pinpricking the window, blurring my view.

I didn't want to go back to the class the following week and thought of saying I wasn't well, but I couldn't face having to explain myself to Catherine and it seemed less bother just to go along. When I arrived, the chairs were set out in rows and everyone was sitting in front of the TV. Margaret gestured to an empty chair next to her at the front but it was too difficult to get past so I sat down in the back row. Mrs Hunter drew the curtains and Cheryl produced a black case, slotted it into the video machine and turned it on. Bright red letters appeared from the corner of the screen, seemed to somersault and rearrange themselves in the centre:

*Zimmerobics With Cheryl!*

The opening bars of 'YMCA' blared out from the speakers and there we were, Zimmers poised. We looked like jellybabies in our tracksuits but, when we started to move, our bodies stretched and kicked and flowed in unison; even our shuffling had a kind of grace. The camera moved round the room, sometimes taking in all of us, sometimes concentrating on one person. There was Edna, with her tongue sticking out, and Alice tutting when she kicked her leg a fraction of a second too late. And finally, right at the end, when I thought they had missed me out, there was I in my green headband, clapping my hands in the air, in perfect time to the music.